self·ish

self·ish

Written By
Dushawn Banks

FINAL DRAFT

This book is a work of fiction. Names, characters, places and incidents are either the product of the author's imagination or used fictitiously, and any resemblance to actual persons, living or dead, events, or locales is entirely coincidental.

Printed in the United States of America

First Printing: November 2019

Banks, Dushawn

Selfish / Dushawn Banks.

ISBN 978-0-578-61156-3

1.Fiction

Book design and composition by Dushawn Banks

PHO·TOG·RA·PHY

/fəˈtägrəfē/

The cover photo of *Selfish* was taken by Dushawn Banks in 2015. It was taken in the beautiful and historic Downtown Savannah, Georgia. Movies such as *Forrest Gump (1994), Gemini Man (2019), Lady and the Tramp (2019), and The Legend of Bagger Vance (2000)* captured similar shots of Downtown Savannah. Though Savannah is a great location for a historic scene, it also is a great location for romance. The cobblestoned streets, beautiful gardens, and historic architecture are perfect for a romantic backdrop. This was captured in the cover photo. It is the Southern version of a historic New York style apartment.

All photos in this book were taken by Dushawn Banks.

CON·TENTS

/kən'tents/

DED·I·CA·TION

/ˌdedəˈkāSH(ə)n/

I dedicate this book to words. Words have allowed us to describe our souls for many years. Though we have been burdened by words, they also helped us in evolution. Words have helped us in love and allows us to express our wants and needs. Words also helped us overcome pain and overstep walls of ignorance. When I think about religious, inspirational, and educational books, I think about the power of words. Knowing this, I'm conscious of the importance of my job. It is the writer who caries cures, recipes, and structure through time. It is the writer who tells the future how to navigate through life. It is the writer who tells the world about love and pain. Knowing this, I am very cautious about my message. Though I know that some may miss the message, there is an intended message.

A great body of work will have many twists and turns, combining reality, actuality, and fantasy. Reality is our version of the world. Actuality is what's actually going on; while fantasy is what we want to happen. In this story there will be highs and lows just like actuality. The writer is not obligated to protect the reader's feelings with suppressing the truth. If we are to successfully learn how to navigate through life, then we should have a proper knowing of the past. Many people argue about the rewriting of history, but they also want their story to be edited. History can't be edited when truth is a factual thing. In order for me to fulfill my intentions of helping generations navigate through young love, I'll have to write an honest story. We've been saturated with the same cliché fantasies, so I'm excited to bring something different to the world.

A book is an intimate space where a writer can talk about the unsaid and I want to give my readers the privilege of reading those unspoken topics. Many people will read the same words different; in that lies the confusion and the beauty. One great thing about writing a body of work is that everyone gets to read it the way that they want to read it. One bad thing about writing a body of work is that everyone gets to read it the way that they want to read it. Some readers will love this book; and others will hate this book. Many readers will be aroused by this book; and many will be enlightened by this book. Some readers will be only entertained by this book, while others will be emotionally connected to this book. Success to a writer is only to make the reader feel something. Whatever the feeling may be, that feeling means that the words translated to the reader's soul. Words can change our soul. That is such a powerful thing.

I say this last because what is said last tends to stay with us the longest. I dedicate this book to women. I say this in the most genuine way that I can on this page. You are the most beautiful thing to ever exist in this world. You are the reason that we all exist. I can name many things that man has built from creations, but I can't name many things that man created. I've always wondered, why are women made so forgiving? Then I realize that she had to be made with love because the continuance of the world is in her hands. Though it may seem like men and women are always at battle, I know that for the sake of the world, we will always find a way to make peace. Judging by my existence, you have never let the world down.

When I asked to get closer to God, I got closer to the woman. I said, "God I don't want any amount of success if it doesn't get me closer to you." When I changed the way that I walked and talked, many people abandoned me; but right there was the woman. She supported every step of my growth. When I asked to get closer to God, I got closer to you. It was you that challenged me to be a great man. It was you that taught me how to love. It was you that gave me a story. It was you that helped me find my purpose. Though we have been through ups-and-downs, no amount of pain could make me ever stop loving you. As a writer, I've had people misunderstand my bad description of a woman. Yes, a woman isn't singular. She is all that I described. What many fail to realize is that when you can love someone beyond the bad times, that shows a deeper level of love. I love you to that level. I hope that I gave you a million smiles for every one time that I made you frown. Thank you, for loving me. Thank you, for trusting me. Thank you, for believing in me. Thank you, for having faith in me. Thank you, for forgiving me. Thank you, for teaching me. Thank you, for supporting me. When I was younger, I didn't understand why I've been surrounded by women my whole life. Now, as a man, I see where that experience helped me with success in relationships. The pillow of love from the women in my life made life easy.

All praise to the 'most-high'. I just want to thank God for giving me talent, love, and intellect. You write my story and I just copy you. I feel as if I'm destined to do this because it is so effortless. I wrote my first script in class when I was fourteen years old and never knew that life would come back full circle. Our intuition knew what we were going to be before our conscious mind knew. I want you to add your grace to these words as they spread throughout the world. Help these words guide the world for generations to come. Help these words find a safe place in the world's heart.

IN·TRO·DUC·TION

/ˌintrəˈdəkSH(ə)n/

One of the most damaging things that we've done to words is limit them to one definition. In our education system we have taught students to take test and come up with one answer for a word; and if they were to think beyond this then they would be punished with failure. Words are broad and can be defined in simplicity or defined extraordinarily. A word like faith has a broad meaning. When we think of faith we may think of believing in a supreme being, but it is much more than that. Faith can be as simple as eating the earth's plants and trusting that they will nourish our bodies. Faith is taking a swim and trusting that the water will carry us. Where have we learned to limit words? My only debate is with the limitations that we put on words and one sided views of the pyramid. What if we only told people that fire burns things? Would we be telling its full abilities, or limiting fire to a singular definition? In return, words limit us. Who are we? Yes, we are a body; but a body is also a heart. A body is also a brain. A body is also water. A body is also cells. A body is also oxygen. Many things make up 'a thing', so many definitions can be used to describe that thing. In defining a thing, words help us get a better understanding, but things can never be fully defined.

Etymology is the tracing of a word back to its origin. For example, the word Ethiopian is formed from the word Ethiop and the suffix – *ian*; which means, *the burned face*. This term was used to describe the people of Africa. So much history is in words. The word selfish contains the word self, plus the suffix, *-ish*. In this case, the word *-ish* is defined as having the characteristics of; and self is used to define a being having an identity. The word self is used as a reflexive pronoun, prefix, and adjective. There are over fifty words in the dictionary containing the word self, so that shows us the versatility of the word. Some positive words include, self-care, self-advancement, self-help, self-devotion, self-defense, self-discipline, self-conscious, self-control, self-awareness, self-expression, self-esteem, self-respect, self-righteous, and self-worth. Some negative words include, self-abuse, self-doubt, self-destruct, and self-hate. With all of these words describing an identity, how did the suffix *-ish* take on the negative version? There isn't a real need for the negative connotation with words existing like self-serving and self-interest.

Language is always changing so the dictionary is always being updated. New words are added and old words are removed. Some words stay the same while other definitions change because of shifts in culture. I think that the word selfish may have been changed over time with culture, because the definition is contradictory to its meaning. How can a person care about themselves and be destructive to the world all in the same definition? To elevate oneself is to elevate the world. To transform oneself is to transform the world. To create an invention for oneself is to create an invention for the world. We love ourselves so much that we tend to love others that look like us. We are able to love others because we see ourselves in others. A mother is more likely to have empathy for another person's child because she sees her child in that child. There are many sororities and fraternities around the world of like-minded individuals.

The balance of being into self is that others give us a purpose. Others give us a reason to think, a reason to love, a reason to believe, and a reason to look forward to tomorrow. There is no self without others. We all exist in relation to something else. We are all created from and continue to exist because of our relation with something else. Even in self-abundance, there is 'but so much' that one can be satisfied with until they became numb. There is only so much food that one can eat in a day. One can only sleep in one house at a time. Even in material wealth; how many times can one buy the same things and continue to be satisfied? When we reach this limit, we will have to find pleasure in pleasing others.

Every country doesn't look at 'self' as a negative term, but conquering self as the greatest achievement. If the origin of many languages is from another language, why can't we define a word from the custom of its origin? Many people have stated on their death bed that they wish that they would have done more for themselves. We are all hopeful, and wish that we can live for many years, but actuality has showed us different. On our death bed we will think about how much that we have built for the world that we will no longer see. How much we have acquired that we can no longer use. The more that I learn of myself, the more I find out that I was never taught about myself. I was never taught my history. I was never taught how to properly nourish my body. I was never taught how to cure and heal myself. I was never taught how to satisfy myself. In learning the history of everyone else, I was unconsciously being taught to put myself last. If indeed we were made in the image of our creator who blessed us with the gift of life; the greatest thing that we can do with this gift is take care of it. To love ourselves is to love what we were made in the image of.

I believe that we can go back to the beginning of the world, start over, and still survive with self-interest. In the jungle, the selfless species will soon meet extinction. I believe that we were created with selfishness in our DNA. This allows us to want to survive. What gives this balance, is love. If all creatures had the power to live a life of negative self-interest, then what makes us want to have kids? What makes us want to create something that we will have to feed and take care of for a number of years? I think that the love for the people that we love is enough to balance the world. That's how even in places of savagery like the jungle, they are still able to continue life. If I stayed on a farm and had a thousand chickens, I have enough to survive on my own. Even if I was self-interested and wanted to exchange my chickens for a taste of a fisherman's fish, the world would still go around in my self-interest. His self-interest worked out for him, just as mine worked out for me.

The world is rotating on balance. Everything is at its perfect balance. When the world is out of balance that's when chaos occurs. We have the perfect balance of men, women, and children. We have the perfect balance of resources. We have the perfect balance of day and night. We have the perfect balance of winter, fall, summer, and spring. We also have the perfect balance of love and self-interest.

The people that questioned the world were the innovators, revolutionaries, inventors, pioneers, philosophers, and creators. If I am made in the image of the creator, who am I not to question the world? If we are all made from the same creator, then who are you to tell me that I can't question the world?

I'm thankful that I've had the opportunity to be selfish. Many people take on responsibility at a young age where they are always needed by others. When they are fresh into adulthood they become a parent, husband, wife, or invested in a consuming career. These roles require them to give themselves to others every minute of the day, without much time for themselves. Even when their actions are at rest, their mind is still focused on everything. Being free is living in a moment without worrying about anything. Many parents are on vacation right now, but their mind is still at home. They are wondering what their child is doing, and often make routine checks to see if they are okay. Taking a break is living life without worrying. Having faith that everything is okay so that your mind can have a break. I have had that moment. I've had the moment where I didn't have to worry about my partner's wants and needs. I've had the moment where I went to sleep and didn't have to worry about if someone was cheating on me. I've had the moment where I didn't have to worry about popular trends or popular materials. I've had the moment where I didn't have to worry about what people thought of me. In this moment, I found out that most of my internal problems came from my relationship with other people. It's so hard not to be affected by the opinions of the world, but I'm so happy that I've gotten to experience peace. Some will never be able to experience it. I found happiness within myself. I'm happy that I know how it feels to be selfish.

This story is written from a man's point of view. At first I wanted to do a well-rounded story from a male and female perspective; but in the constant misunderstanding of each other, being wrong about one another is our reality. Ladies, you always want to know what men are thinking, so here it is. Reality is only perspective, so this is truth in a man's eyes. This is what we think is happening.

-Dushawn Banks

SCREENPLAY READING GUIDE

INT. means interior.

EXT. means exterior.

DAY, NIGHT, AFTERNOON, MORNING, and EVENING is the time of day during the scene, or whether the scene has sunlight or darkness.

[text] is a text message exchange.

INT. DON'S APARTMENT - NIGHT
It is a night scene at Don's apartment.

[laughs] (laughs) a character laughs during, before, or after dialog.

"SELFISH"

Written by

Dushawn Banks

INT. LAX AIRPORT. RESTAURANT - DAY

MICHELLE is at a restaurant reading a brochure that says 'Research in Child Development'. Her smart watch's alarm beeps and has a reminder that says 'FLIGHT'. MICHELLE waves for her waiter and rushes to her flight.

INT. PLANE - DAY

The plane is getting ready for takeoff. The Airline's safety video is playing.

[safety video]
If you have a carry-on, please place it under the seat in front of you. If it won't fit under your seat, please place it in the overhead bin.

MICHELLE pulls out a laptop from her bag and places her luggage under the seat. She opens a file on her laptop that says 'Women in Psychology Speech'.

[safety video]
If you have a hand held device, please switch it to airplane mode.

MICHELLE opens her phone and she is flooded with emails, text, and missed calls. She responds to only one text then puts her phone on airplane mode.

MICHELLE

[Text to Chris]

We're departing now.

[safety video]

In the event that cabin pressure changes, the panels above your seat will open, releasing an oxygen mask. Place the mask over your nose and mouth, pull the elastic strap over your head, and adjust the mask if necessary. Breathing normally, will start the oxygen flow.

MICHELLE plays an album from her media player, puts on her headphones, and closes her eyes.

[music playing]

INT. MICHELLE'S HOUSE. BATHROOM - EVENING

[music playing from before scene]

[safety video's audio]

Be sure to adjust your own mask before helping others.

[water sounds]

MICHELLE is in the tub peacefully taking an oatmeal and milk bath. When she gets out of the tub, she intimately oils her body and combs her hair. She puts on her night clothes and looks at her body from the side in her stand-up mirror.

[music stops] [boom] [door swings open]

MESSIAH

Mama!

MICHELLE straightens up in the mirror and turns toward MESSIAH.

MICHELLE

I'm coming baby. Give mama a minute. Go sit at the dinner table.

MESSIAH

Okay.

INT. MICHELLE'S HOUSE. KITCHEN

[smoke alarm beeping]

MICHELLE runs to take a pot off of the stove.

MICHELLE

Oh no! Please don't be burned!

(Michelle screams)

MICHELLE is cooking rice, baked chicken, corn, and rolls for dinner. MICHELLE poured the top of the rice that was still good into a bowl, and sat the rest to the side. While doing that, the smoke detector was still beeping.

MICHELLE

I'm coming. Shut up!

(Michelle yelled at the smoke detector)

MESSIAH

Shut up!

(Messiah repeated)

MICHELLE

Don't say that baby. That's a bad word.

MESSIAH

Bad!

(Messiah repeats)

INT. MICHELLE'S HOUSE. DINNING ROOM - EVENING

MICHELLE sits at the table while her boys eat. She doesn't have a plate. She just watches them while smiling in amazement.

MICHELLE

Junior let mommy see the phone for a second. I'll let you finish playing the game after you eat.

MICHELLE made a call.

CHRIS

Hello.

MICHELLE

Hey Chris, I'm just getting your missed call. Are you on the way?

CHRIS

I was calling to tell you that I was stopping by the restaurant after work. Melvin needs some help moving some tables. I guess you haven't read my text either.

MICHELLE

No I didn't. Well don't be out all night and come home drunk.

CHRIS

Drunk? That was one time. Are you going to keep bringing that up?

MICHELLE

Just making sure. I'll see you soon.

INT. MICHELLE'S HOUSE. BOYS ROOM - NIGHT

MICHELLE puts the boys in bed.

MICHELLE

Goodnight!

BOYS

Goodnight!

(The boys say in harmony)

INT. MICHELLE'S HOUSE. KITCHEN - NIGHT

MICHELLE removed the burned rice from the pot and poured it in the trash can.

MICHELLE

Yuck!

(Michelle muttered)

The trashcan is full, causing the rice to spill over.

EXT. MICHELLE'S HOUSE. PORCH - NIGHT

MICHELLE puts the trash on the front porch.

INT. MICHELLE'S HOUSE. THEATRE ROOM

MICHELLE sat down in the theater room with a full glass of wine in her hand. She turned on the projector screen.

MICHELLE

Oh, Aiden!
(Michelle sighed in disappointment)

MICHELLE tried to turn on a LCD tablet, but it was dead.

MICHELLE

I guess that this isn't movie night after all.

INT. MICHELLE'S HOUSE. BOY'S ROOM - NIGHT

MICHELLE puts the tablet on the charger and went and peeked at the boys. They were sound asleep. She smiled in the doorway.

INT. MICHELLE'S HOUSE. LIVING ROOM - NIGHT

MICHELLE laid on the couch and browsed the internet on her laptop. She receives a text from her friend ERICA.

MICHELLE

[chuckles]

Erica is so silly.

ERICA

[Text] [picture message]

My face when you don't answer the phone.

MICHELLE

[Text]

Girl, I'm so tired that I can throw this whole phone away. Your hair is cute though. That shirt is cute too.

ERICA

[Text]

Aww! Thanks Girl.

MICHELLE

I'm almost done with that body cream that you brought me for my birthday. I'm addicted now. Where did you get it from? I couldn't find it anywhere.

ERICA

Yes! I need some more too. My brother sells homemade organic skincare products. Well not my real brother, but we're cool. I'll send you a picture. You have seen him before.
[Text] [picture message]

MICHELLE

[Text]
Yeah, I've seen him before. He has some great products. Is he gay or something? Why is he hanging out with you?

ERICA

[Text]
Girl no! He is far from gay. He just has a lot of female friends.

MICHELLE

[Text]
Oh ok. He must be single because my man can't have friends. [angry symbol]

ERICA

[Text]

[laugh symbol]

We all know that. Mine either.

Here is his site.

www.shopdonforbes.com

MICHELLE texted Erica for a couple more minutes. Afterwards she browsed the internet.

MICHELLE

I do need some now. Let me check out his website.

(Michelle whispered to herself)

MICHELLE looked at the site with great interest. She strolled pass a picture of DON and stopped to look at it.

INT. MICHELLE'S HOUSE. LIVING ROOM - MORNING

MICHELLE fell asleep on the couch. She woke up from the sound of music.

[loud music coming from the computer speakers]

MICHELLE opened her eyes and saw CHRIS up making a cup of coffee.

MICHELLE

Good Morning! Why didn't you wake me up last night?

CHRIS

Good Morning! I didn't want to bother you. You looked like you were sleeping well. I did put a cover over you though.

MICHELLE

So what time did you put the cover over me?

MICHELLE gave CHRIS a sarcastic stare.

CHRIS

Ha ha! Really early. (Chris said while smirking and sipping coffee)

MICHELLE glanced at her laptop playing music.

MICHELLE

Can you get the boys ready for daycare while I get dressed?

Mr. Early.

MICHELLE got dressed for work while CHRIS got the boys ready.

[Messiah grabbed her legs]

MESSIAH

Mama!

MICHELLE

Good Morning, Baby.
Baby you're not going to tell your mama Good Morning?
I love you anyway.

AIDEN grumpily sat in silence.

MICHELLE

Mwah!

MICHELLE kissed AIDEN on the cheek.

INT. MICHELLE'S HOUSE. LIVING ROOM - MORNING

MICHELLE walked the kids to the front door and grabbed a cup of coffee before she left.

MICHELLE

Hey, where did you put my laptop? I'm about to go.

CHRIS

It's on the coffee table.

MICHELLE

Did you close the site out? I was looking at some products that I wanted to buy.

CHRIS

I turned the power off. So I guess so.

MICHELLE

Okay. Well then, have a great day at work. We'll see you later.

INT. HOTEL BALLROOM - NIGHT

It's halfway through the night at an annual college alumni party. Every lady is in a fitted dress and every gentlemen is in a dapper tailored suit. Having already greeted every familiar face in the party, MICHELLE and DON finally crossed paths.

MICHELLE

Can you hold my drink? I have to use the ladies room.

MICHELLE gives her friend her drink, and politely rushes through the crowd.

DON says to TONY.

DON

Let's move closer to the dance floor. I think we've seen everything there is to see in this area.

DON and TONY moved through the crowd searching for a new view to see the many beautiful women that were in the building.

Almost to the restroom, MICHELLE stops on a dime, and pauses. Her eyes were locked in a dreamy state. It was like she had forgotten where she was going.

DON'S intuition and senses felt an energy looking at him. When he looked out of the corner of his eyes, it was MICHELLE. He acted as if he didn't see her, but he was just as much 'in aww' as her.

MICHELLE stayed frozen until DON walked out of site.

DON smiled to himself. MICHELLE was just as beautiful as he expected her to be. He didn't know whether she was hiding from him or 'in aww', but he could tell by her body language that there was something there.

FIRST SEX

FIRST SEX
DAY
SCENE
LOCATION
CAST

INT. MICHELLE'S CAR

It's been three months since MICHELLE has come back to her hometown. In these three months, her relationship has been taking unexpected turns. During this time, she hasn't really talked to DON; but on her quiet ride back home she is planning to change that.

NARRATOR
What is the definition of being selfish? It's a beautiful chaos. Every person has a bit of selfishness in them. It keeps us alive by demanding that we take care of self. We are taught that the best individuals give their lives to the world and their family; but what happens when a person decides to focus on self and becomes addicted to the feeling of freedom? Selfishness is a beautiful chaos because selfishness conflicts with a dependent world. One of the most unselfish jobs on earth is being a parent; but who saves the parent? A table-turning time in a relationship is the day that one partner loses fear. Loses fear of the unknown, and the fear of conviction. The day that a person goes out into the world to find something to

save them. Chaos is on the other side of fear; but what happens when a person gets turned on by the chaos? Like a bite to the skin during pleasure; adrenaline adding more doses to the feeling. What happens when a person who once felt weak, finds power in chaos? Finds power in being selfish.

INT. DON'S APARTMENT

DON is at home talking to his friend TONY when he gets a text from his friend ERICA.

ERICA

[Text]

Hey Don! Michelle is in town. She said that she wanted to see you.

DON smiles at his text message and then texts back.

DON

[Text]

Okay, I'm home. When does she want to connect?

ERICA

[Text]

We're headed out for a few drinks, but you can come

to my house when we head
back home.

DON

[Text]

Okay.

DON was reserved in the text, but couldn't believe what he was reading. It was already kind of late which meant that it would be late when he got to ERICA's house. All kind of thoughts were going through his head. He didn't want to jump to conclusions, but it was okay to dream. He had the worse thoughts, but this was a woman that was in a happy relationship. Her partner was a real dapper, clean-cut guy; and he assumed that, that was what most women of her caliber was looking for.

[hours went by]

Midnight came and still no text from ERICA. DON'S hopes had been shattered that quick. He should have known that things just don't fall into your hands that easy. He went to sleep disappointed.

INT. DON'S APARTMENT - MORNING

DON woke up and looked at his phone and saw a text from ERICA.

ERICA

[Text]

Hey, I'm sorry. We ended
up getting too tipsy last
night and fell asleep. You
can come by today when you
get a chance.

DON was thinking, "Yeah that's what I wanted." He knew he had missed the opportunity for anything flirtatious, but he still wanted to be in her presence.

DON

[Text]

Sounds good. I'll text you when I'm on the way.

INT. DON'S CAR - AFTERNOON

DON gets dressed and is on the way to ERICA's house.

DON

[Text]

I'm on the way. I'll be there in 30 minutes.

DON pulled up to ERICA'S house.

DON

[Text]

Outside

ERICA

[Text]

Okay. I'm coming.

ERICA came to the door and greeted DON, and then went upstairs. That was a sign that MICHELLE wanted to spend some personal time with him.
MICHELLE didn't act extremely reserved. They actually felt comfortable with one another.

MICHELLE

I'm sorry. Erica's daughter did something to the T.V this morning and we can't figure out how to fix it. I'll just put some music on, on this laptop.

DON

It's cool. I don't usually look at T.V anyway.

They had conversation over music and occasionally laughed at ERICA'S taste in music. So many songs were hype and they wanted to be chill. MICHELLE found a slow song that they agreed on and put it on repeat.

DON just sat back and kept it cool. He was just studying MICHELLE, getting a feel for her energy. He noticed that when he would look into her eyes she would look away shyly. That let him know that she was really interested in him. He eased himself closer and closer to her. Just close enough to feel her body heat, but not touch. The music was getting to them and as time went by they got more and more comfortable.

They didn't hear from ERICA since DON had arrived. They laughed at the fact that she was in her own world.

MICHELLE

This song is getting me hot. Excuse me! I have to use the restroom.

The guest restroom was a couple feet from them. At that moment DON knew that things could go to the next level at any moment. He figured that she had to wipe the moisture from her panties. His mind was always trying to read her.

MICHELLE came back and sat down.

MICHELLE
I think we need to skip to another song. This song is dangerous.

DON
No, I like this song. Keep playing it.

MICHELLE looked at him and gave a sarcastic smile and they sat in silence.

DON
This song is making me hot too, and now I have to use the restroom.
Come with me....
and bring the laptop.

MICHELLE didn't respond, she just stared at him and walked slowly. She was too shy to admit that she wanted to.

BATHROOM

DON sat on the toilet and MICHELLE sat on his lap staring into space. Her body froze, but her eyes said that she wanted what was about to happen.
DON took the laptop and sat it on the floor, then began to graze his fingertips on MICHELLE's skin. Her body was still frozen, but her eyes were dancing. She was talking with her eyes. She would make facial expressions like DON couldn't see her.
He kissed the back of her neck and then raised her up. He then kissed her lower back, while slowly pulling down her pants. After her pants were down, he pulled down his, puts on a condom, and slowly pulled her body down.

[dramatic soundtrack plays]

The butterflies in her stomach had wings that were spreading at the rhythm of every piano hit. It was like she was jumping out of a plane's door, and to build her confidence, she thought about all of the bad things in her relationship. She had flashbacks of arguments. Nights that CHRIS came in late, and when she was pregnant and vulnerable. When her body got penetrated, is when she jumped out of the plane. She began to see what was on the other side of fear.

She tightened up so it would be hard for him to get in. After a few minutes when he finally got in, he went deeper every stroke.

She didn't make a sound, but began to talk with her eyes. Her eyes got wide. Then she began to look around, thinking with her eyes. Her expression was pleasure, mixed with nervousness, and fear. She made a surprised expression every time that he went deeper. As if she was scared of how far it could go.

DON gave her three extremely hard strokes, and then she stopped him.

MICHELLE stood up.

MICHELLE

Okay! That's enough.

DON didn't say anything.

They gathered themselves, and then went back to the couch.

MICHELLE sat and looked into space, and DON looked at her.

She turned around and looked at him.

MICHELLE

I haven't done that in 5 years.

FIRST NIGHT WITH SOMEONE ELSE

FIRST NIGHT WITH SOMEONE ELSE

DAY

SCENE

LOCATION

CAST

INT. MICHELLE'S CAR - EVENING

MICHELLE is on the highway driving back home. She stopped to check on her kids. They were with their grandmother.

MICHELLE

[phone rings]

DIANNE

Hey girl! Are you back in town?

MICHELLE

No, not yet. I just called to check on the boys. I still have an hour left.

DIANNE

Hold on, let me go get them.

MESSIAH

Mama!

MICHELLE

Hey, Baby. Mama will be home soon. Okay?

MESSIAH

Kay!

MICHELLE

I love you.

MESSIAH

Luh ju!

AIDEN

Hey.

MICHELLE

Hey, Mama big boy. Did you have fun with Grandma?

AIDEN

Yeah.

MICHELLE

I'll see you soon. Love you.

AIDEN

Love you. Bye.

MICHELLE

Give the phone to your Grandma.

DIANNE

Hello.

MICHELLE

I'll be there shortly.

DIANNE

No, Baby! Don't rush. I know you're tired. Just pick them up in the morning before work.

MICHELLE

I'll come get them. It's no problem.

DIANNE
No, Baby! Take a break.

MICHELLE
Okay. I'll see you in the morning.

[hangs up]

[an hour later]

INT. MICHELLE'S HOUSE - NIGHT

MICHELLE walks in the house and does a quick examine of everything. She was looking to see if it was still as clean as she left it, and also if there was a trace of what happened the two days that she was gone.

MICHELLE
[talks to herself]
It's still clean. He probably was gone the whole time knowing him.

MICHELLE took her bags up stairs and unpacked. She was never diagnosed, but always felt like she had OCD. Everything has to be clean. Living in the house with all males, she always finds herself cleaning.

INT. BATHROOM - NIGHT

MICHELLE is in the bathroom running a hot bath. While the water is running, she is looking at herself in the mirror, in her bra and panties. After a few minutes she grabs her phone and sits on the toilet seat.

MICHELLE
[Texting Don]

Hey. I just want you to
know that it was nice
seeing....

MICHELLE stops texting and pauses for a minute. After she paused, she deleted the text. Instead of texting DON, she played the song that she had been playing on repeat at ERICA's house. She smiled as it was playing, and then got in the tub.

INT. LIVING ROOM - NIGHT

CHRIS unlocks the door, and comes in quietly. He looks at the couch and is surprised not to see MICHELLE there. She is always on the couch when he comes home with the television watching her sleep.
He then goes up stairs to see where MICHELLE was. She wasn't in the bedroom, but he could hear music coming from the bathroom.

INT. BATHROOM - NIGHT

MICHELLE soaked in a hot bath, then got out. When she was drying off, she saw her phone light up. The bathroom was dim from the candlelight, so the phone shined bright. She had a new text from ERICA and DON.

DON

[Text]
Hey Beautiful. I was
checking to see if you
made it home safe.

DON didn't know how she felt about what happened so he just refrained from talking about it.

MICHELLE

[Text]

Hey, Handsome. I am home now, getting ready for bed. I had a great time as well.

DON

[Text]

That's great. Goodnight. ♥

MICHELLE

[Text]

♥ Goodnight, Sir.

MICHELLE talks to herself.

MICHELLE

Erica, I will talk to you tomorrow. I am tired honey.

MICHELLE opens the bathroom door, and soon as she steps out, she sees CHRIS.

CHRIS

Where are the boys?

MICHELLE jumped because she didn't hear him come in. MICHELLE held her heart, then gathered herself.

MICHELLE

They are at your mom's house. She told me to pick them up in the morning.

CHRIS

Oh okay!
How is your mom doing?

MICHELLE

Everyone is good.
(Michelle said while
walking away.)

CHRIS never asked about her mom, so she wasn't going to give him the time to carry on a conversation about her trip.

MICHELE went to the bedroom and put on some night clothes. She covered all the way up with some sweatpants and an old t-shirt from her high school. Even though her and CHRIS wasn't on good terms, she didn't want there to be a chance of him touching her.
CHRIS took a shower then came back to the bedroom.
He got in bed and then grabbed MICHELLE, and pulled her close to him.
MICHELLE woke up.

MICHELLE

Mm mm! (a mumbled no) It's
too hot for that.

MICHELLE turned over and CHRIS did the same.

INT. KITCHEN - MORNING

MICHELLE

Good Morning to you too.
(She said sarcastically
while walking pass Chris)

CHRIS

Good Morning.
(Chris said in an
unenthusiastic voice)

MICHELLE

I just want you to know that we're still not on good terms so don't try to touch me while I'm sleeping.

Before CHRIS got a chance to say anything MICHELLE walked out of the front door.

INT. MICHELLE'S CAR - MORNING

Every morning before MICHELLE went to work, she dropped the boys off to daycare.

INT. DIANNE'S HOUSE - MORNING

MICHELLE pulled up to DIANNE'S house and the boys came outside. Her eyes lit up. She got excited every time she saw her boys.

MICHELLE

Thank you for keeping the boys.
(Michelle said to Dianne)
Tell your Grandma bye.
(Michelle said to the boys)

MESSIAH & AIDEN

Byeeeeee!

DIANNE

Bye, Babies!
(Dianne said to the boys)
How are you and Chris doing?
(Dianne said to Michelle)

MICHELLE
We're doing okay.

DIANNE
That's good.
Well I'll see you later.

Even though MICHELLE and CHRIS weren't doing so well, she loved his mom. She had too much respect for her to tell her otherwise.
She dropped the boys off to daycare and headed to work.

[later]

INT. DON'S APARTMENT - NIGHT

DON is at home cooking dinner when he gets a random text from MICHELLE. They rarely talk so this text is a total surprise.

MICHELLE
[Text]
Why don't you ever ask me anything? You don't know where I work, what I'm going to school for, or anything else.

DON
[Text]
I'm sorry. I was sort of minding my business. I didn't know that I could text you. I don't know what you have going on at home.

MICHELLE

[Text]

What do you mean? I don't have anything going on.

DON

[Text]

Well the next time you're in town we can talk all day. I'll be sure to ask you everything.

MICHELLE

[Text]

Okay! I'll be there this weekend.

The week went by and MICHELLE was on the way to DON's apartment. This was her first time over so he made sure that he impressed her with dinner.

MICHELLE

[Text]

What's the code to the gate?

DON

[Text]

0801

Apartment 713

MICHELLE parked her car and checked herself in the visor mirror. She touched up her hair and sprayed perfume. Then when she felt ready, she grabbed her overnight bag and headed to the door.

[Door Knocks]

DON

[opens door]
It was unlocked.

MICHELLE

I don't just walk into people's place.

DON

You look beautiful. So you're not going to give me a hug?

MICHELLE walks past DON, puts her bag down, and comes back for a hug. She really wanted to hug him to begin with, but she had to play nonchalant. She was definitely excited to finally be at his place; and she missed him.

DON

Mmm! You smell good.

MICHELLE

Thanks. No, that food smells good. What are you cooking?

DON

Lemon pepper salmon, mash potatoes, and asparagus.

MICHELLE

That sounds good.

MICHELLE and DON ate dinner with a glass of wine. Then after dinner, they laid on the living room floor finishing the rest of the bottle. They laid there and talked for four hours straight. DON was impressed by her knowledge. He found out that she was a psychology major so she joined in with him on deep topics. He had judged her and didn't expect much. She was so beautiful that he thought that she was just another pretty face. Now he was intrigued. They had many similarities. Both were from a big family. Both came from humble beginnings, but strived for more.

[train passes by]

DON

I hate that train. They didn't tell me that I was staying next to a train track before I moved in.

MICHELLE

I like the train. It makes me feel like I'm somewhere different. You know when you are running behind kids all week it feels good when you're away. I like it here.

DON

Are you married? Somehow I brought up your name to someone and they asked if you were still married. I think I told them that I sold you a cream.

MICHELLE

No! People may think that because I don't put my life on display. I'm not married. It's a long story. I'll tell you one day, but I like to keep my personal life to myself.

Especially when it
involves other people.

DON

Oh okay! I was kind of mad too. I was like, why didn't she tell me? I don't mess around with married people.

MICHELLE stopped talking for a while. For about 15 minutes, she had tuned DON out and was just staring into his eyes. She noticed that his eyes where really beautiful in this moment of silence. She was falling for his nonchalant, laidback confidence. She is a beautiful woman that usually has the upper hand with men. She had many men chasing her, but it was something about the one who didn't. She wondered why did it bother her so much that he wasn't trying to get to know her before. She quickly came back to reality when DON changed the subject.

DON

You know that I saw your sons father at the party. He was staring at me. It was strange.

MICHELLE

For real? I wonder why did he do that.

Though DON didn't say it, his intuition told him that he knew exactly who he was. He could tell that they may have had a conversation about him. He knew what that stare meant, because he too had been on that side of the fence. He didn't want to ask too many questions about another man so he kept the questions minimal; but he still didn't fully trust her story. He knew that she was leaving a lot out. Even with wanting to know more, he knew that he had to respect her privacy.

FIRST FEBRUARY

FIRST FEBRUARY

DAY

SCENE

LOCATION

CAST

It was Valentines morning and the guys were stretching before they ran a trail, and talking about the day ahead.

MALIK

What did you'll get for Valentines? I spent so much money. I had to buy something for my wife, my daughter, and the ladies at work.
Well, I didn't have to, but you know I like to put a smile on their faces.

[laughs]

CHAD

You're funny. You just like to be called Boss.

MALIK

Hell yeah. You know I love that. Some women are so happy for little gifts. These dudes out here are delusional. Some of them told me that they have never received a gift in their lives.

CHAD

Man I have to buy two gifts. It's a long story.

[laughs]

DON

Damn! This is my first year free. I spent so much

money last year, but you
know I love it too.

JOSH interrupted the conversation. He was just their running partner. They didn't know much about him outside of the trail.

JOSH

I didn't buy anything. My
girl doesn't care about
things like that.

DON and MALIK reacted at the same time. CHAD put his head down.

MALIK

What?

JOSH

My girl said that she
doesn't care about that.
I'm serious.

MALIK

... and you fell for that?

DON

Don't care about what? The
biggest holiday of the
year for a woman! Women
will even skip Christmas
and let it be about the
kids before they skip
Valentines. She may not
even be mad about the
gifts, but she will be by
the time all of her
friends call bragging
about their day. Plus,
it's going to be

embarrassing for her to
say that you didn't do
anything for her.
Man, I'm going to tell you
like this; and don't take
this as disrespect.
Somebody is going to have
sex with your girl after
that.
... and that's just real.

CHAD

Don't tell that to him
like that!!

JOSH

Yeah, I hear you, but my
girl is different.

DON

Alright, then.

They finished the trail and headed home to get ready for the big day.

INT. DON'S CAR - AFTERNOON

An hour after they left the trail, DON called MALIK.

DON

What's up MALIK? I stopped
by the store after the
trail, and guess who I see
at the store buying roses
and a teddy bear?

MALIK

Who?

DON

Josh!

MALIK

(hysterically laughing)

DON

I don't get why dudes try to act so hard. You'll be crying when the next man gets a hold of her. You know I know his girl. She used to want me. I really was speaking truth.

(laughs)

MALIK

(laughing)

Oh, Man! I'm happy that I'm married.

DON

I'll talk to you tomorrow. Enjoy your Valentines, and don't make any more babies. Give me a chance to make one.

(laughs)

MALIK

I don't know man. I got a nice condo tonight.

...and how big that tub is, some things might happen.

(laughs)

[hangs up]

DON hangs up and starts thinking about Valentines. All of his friends were busy today, so it was just him. He texted MICHELLE at a red light.

DON

[Text]
Happy Valentines,
Beautiful. ♥♥♥

MICHELLE

[Text]
Thanks. ♥
I really appreciate that.

DON

[Text]
Call me later if you get a chance.

MICHELLE

[Text]
Okay.

DON sat in the house for the rest of the night while everyone else painted the town red. Every restaurant, theatre, and hotel was filled. They had a concert going on as well. DON sat and watched the festivities from his phone. While looking online, he saw a picture of MICHELLE dressed up really nice. She looked beautiful. By the way that she was dressed, he could tell that she was headed out on a date.

INT. DON'S APARTMENT - AFTERNOON

DON gets a call from MALIK.

MALIK

A man, I need you to come check out this car with me. My wife set up an appointment for me to check out this Corvette that ABE Motors just got in. We can ride together. If I like it enough, we may pull off today.

[laughs]

DON

Ha ha! Man you're married, you don't need that car. Give it to some brothers that know how to use it. I'll be ready when you are.

MALIK came and got DON, and they headed over to the car lot.

INT. ABE LUXURY MOTORS SHOWROOM - AFTERNOON

RECEPTIONIST

Hi! Welcome to ABE Luxury Motors. How may I assist you?

MALIK

Hi! I have an appointment today. My name is Malik Williams.

The RECEPTIONIST looked at her computer to check the appointment.

RECEPTIONIST

You can have a seat Mr. Williams. Would you gentlemen like a glass of champagne while you are waiting?

MALIK

Yes. That would be great.

MALIK and DON sits in the lobby and wait for their salesman. Instead, the General Manager came over.

JOHN

Good Afternoon, Mr. Williams. I’m John Hines. The General Manager. So you wanted to check out the Corvette! We just got it in. It’s a beauty.

MALIK

Yes, indeed!

JOHN

Well, you gentlemen can take a walk with me.

DON and MALIK took a look at the Corvette. DON went and took a call, while MALIK finished up.

MALIK

We’ll definitely keep in touch. Once I close on this house, I’ll be ready to come get her.

JOHN

I'm going to let you talk to my sales consultant. She just came back from lunch. Her office is over here.

JOHN and MALIK walked in the SALE CONSULTANT's office.

JOHN

Amber. This is Malik Williams. Can you further assist Mr. Williams?

AMBER reaches out for a handshake.

AMBER

Nice to meet you Mr. Williams.

MALIK shook AMBER'S hand and smiled. He smiled in salutation, but also because he knew that DON was going to love her.

After a few minutes JOHN walked DON to AMBER'S office. DON sat down next to MALIK and gave him a look showing his interest.

AMBER was looking down at some papers and raised her head and saw DON.

AMBER

[quick stutter]
H-How are you?

DON

Hi!
(Stares into her eyes with focus)

DON was very observant. When AMBER lifted her head, her eyes gave DON a look of lust. He kind of figured that he was jumping to conclusions, but he didn't know for sure.

DON gave AMBER no emotion, but he looked straight into her eyes the whole time. She was beautiful. She was dressed in professional attire, but when she came back from lunch, she had a pink and green sorority jacket on. That told DON that it was more to her, and he wanted to find out.

DON stayed quiet the whole time, while MALIK wrapped up. He was a pretty reserved person anyway.

When leaving, AMBER shook both of the guys hands again.

AMBER

Mr. Williams I'll see you very soon.

... and Mr....

(paused waiting for Don to answer)

DON

Forbes. Don Forbes.

AMBER

Well, Mr. Forbes, I hope to see you soon as well. Maybe, I can get you into something.

DON

I would love to, but I just bought one messing around with Malik. I'm not really flashy.

AMBER

You look like a man of style. It's just stylish, not flashy.

INT. MALIK'S CAR - AFTERNOON

DON

Damn! She was beautiful. Now that's my type right there. That's all I need.

MALIK

Yeah, she was nice.

DON

I'll marry something like that.

MALIK

Well, it's about that time my brother.
You'll be thirty in a couple of years.
... and then you'll be buying a house like me.
I'm so ready to get that Corvette, but I have to make sure the wife gets what she wants first. It's true what they say.
Happy wife, happy life.

DON

Why not happy husband, happy life too?

(Don laughs)

You're lucky that you found yours early. It's tough out here these days.

MALIK

Yeah! Marriage isn't easy, but it's worth it. I found

mine early and I couldn't
let her get away.

[two days later]

INT. DON'S APARTMENT - NIGHT

DON was at home checking his daily orders from his e-commerce site, when he ran across a familiar name. AMBER MONROE. He was excited and shocked. His senses were right, and she made the first move. He didn't know whether it was crazy or spontaneous that she found him; but he didn't care. He sent her a personal confirmation email. He also asked would she like her order to be shipped or picked up.

When she chose for her order to be picked up, DON offered to drop it off.

DON was excited because, not only was she his type, they had mutual interest. He was never the type to force anything. He believed that the best things happen on their own.

EXT. ABE LUXURY MOTORS - AFTERNOON

DON pulled up to AMBER'S job on her lunch break and brought her order. He was taking a gamble, but he also brought her a plate of food that he had cooked.

AMBER

Hi, there! Thank you, so
much.

DON

No, Thank You!
I got you something
else...
... so you can stop eating
that fast food.

AMBER

... and you can cook.
Thanks!
Spoiling me already. Don't start nothing that you can't finish.

DON

Ha ha! I cook every day.
No pressure.

AMBER

We'll see. I'm going to run back inside. I'll talk to you later.

DON

Okay. Later.

DON knew that this was the beginning of something and he hoped that she was the one.

FIRST SPRING

FIRST SPRING

DAY

SCENE

LOCATION

CAST

INT. MICHELLE'S HOUSE - NIGHT

MICHELLE just finished cooking dinner. The kids were eating while she cleaned up the kitchen.

MESSIAH

Mama! I'm finished.

MICHELLE walks over to the table.

MICHELLE

No, you're not. Finish your food so you can grow into a big boy.
You want to be a big boy Messiah?

MESSIAH

Yes.

MICHELLE

Okay then, eat your food, and then you can come go to sleep with Mama.

CHRIS walks in and joins the conversation.

CHRIS

Why do they have to sleep with us every night?
You're starting something.
Now they are going to want to be there every night.

MICHELLE gives CHRIS a sarcastic look.

MICHELLE

That's cool.

My babies can stay as long as they want.

CHRIS gives back a demanding look.

CHRIS

Oh, okay. We'll see.

MICHELLE

What do you mean by 'we'll see'? You're not kicking my babies out.

MICHELLE knew why CHRIS didn't want the boys in the room, but she used them to stay distant.

MICHELLE

I told you that I didn't want to do anything for Valentines, but you wanted to go out.

CHRIS

Valentines?

(Chris yelled)

MICHELLE

Don't yell in front of my kids.

(While raising a brow)

CHRIS

What makes you think I care about Valentines?

(Chris said in a lower tone)

MICHELLE

I'm just saying.

CHRIS walks off in defeat because he couldn't say too much in front of the kids.

INT. MICHELLE'S HOUSE - MORNING

It was a usual weekday morning at MICHELLE'S house. She got the kids ready and prepared morning snacks. When she was ready to head out of the door, she remembered that she had to get some money for the kids.

INT. BATHROOM - MORNING

MICHELLE stood at the door while CHRIS tied his tie in the mirror.

MICHELLE

Hey, I need the money for the boys' shoes so I can get them after I leave work.

CHRIS

What money?

MICHELLE

Huh! The shoes that we talked about.
(Michelle said in shock)

CHRIS

I don't know what you're talking about, but you can take care of it.

MICHELLE

I don't have time to play with you. I'm about to be late.

(Michelle rolled her eyes
and walked off)

CHRIS found his own way to strike back.

INT. MICHELLE'S CAR - MORNING

MICHELLE dropped the boys off to daycare and headed to work. On her way, she received a call from ERICA.

MICHELLE
[phone rings]
Hey Girl.
(talking through the car's
Bluetooth audio)

ERICA
Hey. I just got your text.
What is Chris tripping
about now?

MICHELLE
I guess that he is trying
to get me mad by not
buying the kids' shoes.
... but you get mad at me
and take it out on 'your'
kids?
That's okay though,
because my kids will
always have everything
that they need.
... and that's why I'm
starting my Masters this
year. You can't depend on
a man. They will always
find a way to take from
you when they get mad.

ERICA

Amen! You see what
happened to Megan.

MICHELLE

Yeah, but she put herself
in that position.

ERICA

Just ask Don to buy the
shoes.

(Erica chuckles)

MICHELLE

Girl, please! Them aren't
his kids. I'm not doing
that.
Plus, I'm about to stop
messing with him anyway.
He is too inconsistent for
me. It's so crazy that you
can have a million dudes
lined up waiting on you
and the one that you give
a chance, takes it for
granted.
I'm about to answer some
of these messages that I
have piled up.
(Michelle laughs)
I know some that will
gladly buy the shoes.

ERICA

Especially, Damon.

MICHELLE

Oh, My God.
(Michelle laughs)

Girl, Bye.

INT. DON'S APARTMENT - NIGHT

DON was at home when he received a text from AMBER.

AMBER

[Text]
The food was great Mr. Forbes.
It's too late, I'm spoiled. [tongue symbol]

DON

[Text]
Thanks, my dear. Well, I guess that I just gained another job.

AMBER

[Text]
Yes, you have. Why aren't you married cooking like this?

DON

[Text]
If marriage was that simple, I think plenty of people would be. Maybe I was waiting on you.

AMBER

[Text]
Maybe. [blush symbol]

DON

[Text]

I don't have to cook for you to feed you. Let's do lunch tomorrow.

AMBER

[Text]

Sounds good to me.

DON

[Text]

What time is your lunch break?

AMBER

[Text]

I usually take it around 12 o'clock.

DON

[Text]

Well, twelve it is.

EXT. ABE LUXURY MOTORS - AFTERNOON

DON pulled up to AMBER'S job and she was waiting for him in the parking lot. When he pulled up, she sat still, and waited for him to come open her door.

DON

What the hell is this girl doing?

(Mumbling to himself)

Oh! I'm tripping.

DON gets out of the car and goes around to open the door.

DON

So you're waiting on me
huh?
Here you go Miss Lady.

AMBER

I was about to leave you
out here.

AMBER gets into the car and they drive to a close restaurant.

INT. RESTAURANT - AFTERNOON

DON and AMBER are settled inside of the restaurant having conversation over lunch.

AMBER

I love your website. I'm
going to try your products
in Miami this weekend. Me
and my sorority sisters
are having a girls' trip.

DON

Thanks. I designed my site
myself.
...and that trip sounds
like fun. Me and the
fellas need to take a
guys' trip.

AMBER

So how long have you been
making natural products?

DON

This is my first year. I
started with a cream and

people loved it, so I started doing more. I wouldn't say that it's a passion. It's just a way to make money for me.

AMBER

So you're like a Jack of all trades huh? What else do you do?

DON

You'll just have to wait and see. I like to surprise. I can't tell you everything.
So tell me a little about you?

AMBER

Well. I graduated from Spelman with a Bachelor of Economics. I'm working on my Masters now. I do hair, volunteer, and coach a cheerleading team.

DON

Very impressive. I guess that you are the Jane of all trades.
[laughs]

DON and AMBER continued to get to know each other until it was time for AMBER to go back to work.

INT. DON'S APARTMENT - AFTERNOON

[days later]

AMBER
[Text] [picture message]

AMBER sent DON a picture of her putting on his cream.

DON
[Text]
♥ So Beautiful! Thanks.
I'm going to post that
right now.

AMBER
[Text]
Awww! ♥

DON
[Text]
Have fun. I'll talk to you
later.

AMBER
[Text]
Okay.

DON forwards the picture to his sister.

DON
[Text] [picture message]
So what do you think about
her?

SIERRA
[Text]
♥♥♥ She is beautiful.
Where did you find her at?

DON

[Text]

[laugh symbol] Around. She seems pretty cool. I'm going to see where it goes.

SIERRA

[Text]

If you want me to do an investigation on her I will. [wink symbol]

DON

[Text]

No that's okay. She's not from here.

DON posted the picture on his social media site with the caption [trophy symbol]

INT. ERICA'S HOUSE - NIGHT

ERICA was browsing her social media page when she saw DON'S picture of AMBER posted. She texted MICHELLE.

ERICA

[Text]

When was the last time that you talked to Don?

MICHELLE

[Text]

It's been a while. Why what's up?

ERICA

[Text]

I think that he might have
a girlfriend now. Go look
at his page.

MICHELLE looks at DON's post.

MICHELLE

[Text]
Well, she's pretty. There
is no telling with him.
I'm happy for him.

ERICA

[Text]
Oh, Okay. Just making sure
that you saw it.

[two weeks later]

INT. SEVANANDA NAUTURAL FOODS MARKET - NIGHT

DON is walking around a grocery store that he pulled over to, talking to MALIK. He was supposed to be on the way to pick up AMBER for a date, but hasn't heard from her since they set the date up. She stayed in a nearby city and he didn't have the address to get there.

DON makes a call.

MALIK

Hello.

DON

What's up Malik?
I want to get your opinion
on something because I
don't know if I'm thinking
wrong.

I'm thinking about leaving Amber alone. We were supposed to be going on a date tonight and she just stopped answering the phone. She is the one that planned the date.
The only thing that I could think of is that she has a man.
She is just trying to be too perfect. She acts like she does nothing wrong. Plus, she makes me open her car door all of the time. That's just too much. I'll open doors, but damn. The car door is too much.

MALIK

[laughs]
Man I think that you're jumping to conclusions. If she is used to a man opening car doors for her then that is just the price that you have to pay to date her. My wife doesn't require that, but every woman is different.

DON

I don't know man. I can't take anymore loses.

MALIK

I'm going to tell you like this. Messing with love

you may lose; and that's
the catch.
... but you won't find
love being scared to lose.

DON

Yeah, you're right. I
can't even lie. I'm scared
to lose, but I guess that
comes with it. I'm just
going to calm down and
wait on her explanation.
... Alright, appreciate
it.

MALIK

Alright.
[hangs up]

INT. GYM - AFTERNOON
[a month later]

DON and his friend TONY is at his apartment's gym working out. DON is bench pressing, while TONY spots him.

TONY

5,6,7,8...Come on. Two
more. 9...10.

DON

Aaahh!
(Don screams in
exhaustion)
Man, that's it for me.

TONY

I can't believe this that
girl got you lifting

weights. As long as I knew you, you never stayed consistent in the gym.

DON

Well, it's a time for everything.

TONY

You're turning into a husband, I see.

DON

Hey, man! You have to give the game up some day.

DON shrugs.

DON

Man, I don't know what kind of book that she read, but she is really about to make me wait 90 days. She lets me kiss on her and do everything else, but go all the way. I know one thing; she better be consistent. If you're going to act perfect, then you better play that role forever. I'm not even into the perfect thing; but then again we do love lies.

TONY

Damn! You're better than me, because she would've

been waiting 90 days by
herself.

[laughs]

Alright. I'm about to head
out. I'll catch up with
you later.

EXT. DOWNTOWN - NIGHT

DON, TONY, MALIK, and CHAD are leaving a club when they run into a group of girls that they know.

DOWNTOWN GIRL 1

Hey! I haven't seen you
guys in so long.
(While hugging the guys)

DON and CHAD walks off to talk to two of her friends.

DOWNTOWN GIRL 2

They shut the club down
early and it's my friend's
birthday. We're trying to
party all night.

CHAD

What are you all trying to
do?

DOWNTOWN GIRL 2

I don't know. We may go
back to my house and play
cards. You and Don should
come. My friend likes him
anyway.

DON

Okay, that's cool. We'll call you when we leave here.

After they finished the conversation, DON and CHAD meets back up with TONY and MALIK.

MALIK

Well, fellas. I'm about to head home. My time is up. I'll see you guys in a couple months.

(laughs)

DON

Alright. We're probably going to be up all night. We're going to meet up with them.

MALIK

Alright. Don't get caught up. I don't want to hear you crying about not being able to find a good woman if you mess this one up.

DON

(laughs)

Yeah. You're right. I won't do anything crazy.

INT. DON'S APARTMENT - NIGHT

DON is at home talking to his sister on the phone.

SIERRA

Hey. What are you doing?

DON

Waiting on Amber. I'm wrapping her gift up so I can hide it. Tomorrow is her birthday.

SIERRA

Awww! That's sweet. Mom said that she doesn't like her.

DON

Huh! How is she going to not like someone that she doesn't know? Where did she see her?

SIERRA

I sent her picture to everybody in a group text. She said that you need to be careful. You know Mom doesn't like pretty girls.

DON

Yeah! She's tripping.

DON set up a romantic vibe in the living room. He lit candles, sprinkled rose petals, and played a smooth soundtrack. He took the living room table and used it for the food. Instead of chairs, he put blankets and pillows on the floor.

[door knocks]

AMBER

Hello.

DON

Happy Birthday.

AMBER

Thank you. It looks beautiful in here.

DON brought dinner out and they sat and had conversation.

AMBER

So, do you do this for every woman?

DON

Huh! That's the first thing that you think of when a man does something nice for you?

(Don says sarcastically)

AMBER

I'm just asking. You never know.

DON

The ones that I like.
... but I rarely like, so I guess that you're lucky.

AMBER

I guess that I am.

They finished dinner and things got a little heated. DON was kissing on her as usual, but this time she was a little more open.

DON took a shower and came back to the room in a towel. AMBER was laying on the bed.

DON

Would you get my back?

(Don said while handing Amber a bottle of skin moisturizer)

AMBER rubbed DON'S back and then quickly stopped.

DON

What happened to that back massage that you owe me?

AMBER

You mean the one that you owe me?

DON

I'll get you after.

AMBER

Okay, lay down.

DON laid on his stomach while AMBER sat on his lower back. Though he thought that she was purposely giving a basic massage, he was happy to be touched by her. He could feel heat coming from in between her legs, warming his lower back. He could also feel the surface of her vagina and immediately got erect. He knew that he couldn't lay on his stomach for too long because it was uncomfortable with an erection so hard. He lifted up a bit pressing his lower back against her clitoris creating stimulation.

DON

Okay. Let me do you now.

(Don said while getting
up)

DON flipped AMBER over and began to massage her back. His intentions were to stimulate and not massage. Once he rubbed in most of the moisturizer, he rubbed his fingertips across her back. Then he rubbed his face passionately across her back, followed by his lips. He rubbed his lips across her skin, and every five seconds, stopped to kiss her back. After a few minutes, he pressed his erection up against her. She moaned. He then turned her back around and spread her legs wide open until they couldn't open anymore. He laid his body inside of her legs and continued to passionately kiss her. He took his fingers and pressed them against her clitoris while he kissed her. He then slid her panties down. He rubbed the head of his penis onto her clitoris for a few minutes then put on a condom. When he was ready to put it in, AMBER got tense. He put his head in and she moaned in pain. She was uncomfortably tight, so DON took it really slow. He got his penis halfway in and pulled back. He knew that she wasn't ready for the whole thing, so he was patient. After about ten minutes, DON stopped. He didn't really get any pleasure out of the sex; he just wanted to open the doors for the future.

INT. DON'S APARTMENT.KITCHEN - MORNING

DON prepared a birthday breakfast while AMBER was sleep. He set up two plates for her. One had steak and eggs on it, and the other had a waffle topped with strawberries. He poured pineapple juice inside of a wine glass, with diced strawberries inside. Then he placed a dozen red roses on the side of the plate with her gift. After everything was set up, he took a picture and posted it on his social media page. The caption read, Happy Birthday @amber_1908 [heart sign]. That was his way of making things more official.

EXT. DRIVEWAY - MORNING

MALIK and DON were washing their cars at MALIK'S house.

DON

A Malik. You ever feel like things are going too good in your life?

(He said while washing the car)

DON walks closer to MALIK.

DON

I just feel like things are going too good for me now. Like something bad is just bound to happen. I guess that when all you know is pain, happiness feels strange.

MALIK

You just have to accept that you're blessed. That you're a good person, so you deserve what the world gives you back.

DON

Yeah, I guess so.

FIRST SUMMER

FIRST SUMMER

DAY

SCENE

LOCATION

CAST

INT. DON'S APARTMENT - MORNING

DON wakes up and checks his phone. He then gives AMBER a text.

DON

[Text]

Good Morning, beautiful. What happened to you calling me back last night?

AMBER

[Text]

I did call you back last night. What do you mean?

DON

[Text]

I didn't get it.

AMBER

[Text]

So are you calling me a liar?

DON

[Text]

No. I'm just saying that I didn't get it.

AMBER

[Text]

Okay, since I'm a liar. Then don't call me anymore.

DON stops texting and calls AMBER three times and she doesn't answer.

Don

[Text]

????

AMBER doesn’t text back and DON doesn’t text back either.

INT. BAR - NIGHT

DON, CHAD, and TONY is at a bar having drinks.

TONY

Let’s have a toast to Don being back out here in the streets with us.

(Tony laughs)

That was the quickest relationship that I ever saw.

CHAD shakes his head.

CHAD

So, she didn’t tell you why she is mad with you?

DON

I’ve been around long enough to know that, that was an intentional break up. Her ex might have come back into her life or something. You never know. There is no need to fight it. It is what it is. All I can say is that I tried. Now I’m back out here.

(Don says in disappointment)

CHAD

Have you talked to Michelle lately?

DON

Not really. I texted her on her birthday. I saw that she went to Vegas. I guess that her and her old man is back on good terms.

CHAD

I don’t understand women. They will leave a dude, then go right back. What’s the point in leaving?

DON

Because women need constant attention. They act like they are scared to be alone. That’s the scary part. If you all take a break, you better believe that she’s going to start a relationship with someone else quick.

TONY waves to the bartender.

TONY

Can we all get another round.

Don did you see that Shannon announced that she was pregnant?

DON

Yeah. I saw that.

CHAD

Damn. You guys just broke up not too long ago.

DON

Yeah, that's what she wanted. I wanted her to finish school first, but I hope that she's happy.

TONY

Damn, he wasn't playing.

DON

I'm having kids when I'm ready. I'm not letting anybody rush me. There are too many people blaming their kids for things that they didn't accomplish. I'm not going to be like that. I have some more things to accomplish.

CHAD

Hell Yeah.

[2 months later]

INT. FARMER'S MARKET - AFTERNOON

DON is at a Farmer's Market preparing to cook dinner for a small gathering. He calls some close friends to tell them about his plan.

DON

[phone rings]

ERICA

Hello.

DON

What's up? I'm cooking dinner tonight. You and your sisters can come through if you all want to.

ERICA

Sounds good. I'll be there. I'm going to call them, then I'll let you know.

INT. DON'S APARTMENT - EVENING

DON is at home preparing for his dinner gathering when he receives a text from ERICA.

ERICA

[Text]
What time do you want us to come? Angel and Jasmine said that they are coming.

DON

[Text]
8 should be good.

ERICA

[Text]
Okay, Michelle wanted to know if can she come too?

DON

[Text]

I didn't know that she was in town. Of course.
(He texted smiling at his phone.)

ERICA

[Text]
I'll let her know. See you soon.

TONY and CHAD was the first guest to arrive. MALIK came by himself shortly after. JASMINE and ANGEL came together; and ERICA and MICHELLE came together.

TONY let's everyone in while DON is cooking.

INT. DON'S APARTMENT. KITCHEN - NIGHT

DON sets up the dinner plates on the kitchen counter and calls everyone to come eat.

JASMINE

This looks so good.
(Jasmine says grabbing her plate.)

ANGEL

Thank you, Don.

ERICA

Thank you, sir.

MICHELLE shyly creeps up after ERICA. This was her and DON's first close interaction since she arrived. DON starred into her eyes as she approached, and she blushed.

DON

Hold up, let me make sure that this plate is perfect.

MICHELLE

(Michelle giggled)

Thank you. I missed your cooking.

DON

Oh, so you don't miss me?

(Don said sarcastically)

MICHELLE smiled and walked away.

INT. DON'S APARTMENT. LIVING ROOM - NIGHT

JASMINE

That was so good Don. You have to teach me that recipe.

DON

Thank you, ma'am. Anytime. Just let me know when you're ready. It's simple.

ANGEL

That's a shame that a man can cook better than us.

ERICA

Girl, I'm telling you!

ANGEL

I'm trying to learn how to cook a few of those recipes for my man.

DON walked around and gathered all of the plates and took them to the kitchen. MICHELLE got up and followed him.

INT. DON'S APARTMENT. KITCHEN - NIGHT

MICHELLE

I'll wash them. You've done enough.

DON

Okay. Thanks.

INT. DON'S APARTMENT. LIVING ROOM - NIGHT

The night has moved along and everyone is in the living room having a casual discussion over drinks. Everyone is more vocal, due to the influence of the drinks.

ERICA

Men just don't get it sometimes. Women are attracted to things that they don't think about.

MICHELLE

Right! A woman with kids loves to see a man taking care of his kids. That's sexy as hell.

ERICA.ANGEL.JASMINE

(Make sounds of agreement)

CHAD

But, what if he doesn't have kids?

MICHELLE
Then that's even better. Then we won't have to deal with drama. There are other ways that we can find out what type of man we're dealing with.

DON
Oh! So you all study us?

ERICA
Yes!
(Erica says while looking at Michelle.)

MICHELLE smirks.

MICHELLE
And, we love a man that can cook.
(Michelle says while staring at Don and drinking out of her wine glass.)

DON smiles.

DON
We like psychologist. That's sexy as hell.

ERICA
Well, I'm not a psychologist, but I'll take some more of this wine.
(Erica says while getting up.)

This is my favorite wine
too.
(Erica says while looking
at the bottle.)

MALIK gets up and shakes DON's hand.

MALIK
Well my brother it's time
for me to roll.

DON
Alright, man. Let me walk
you to the car.

EXT. DON'S APARTMENT. PARKING LOT - NIGHT

DON walks MALIK to his car laughing at some of the discussions that were made earlier.

DON
[laughs]
Women are so funny.

MALIK
[laughs]
Yes, they are.
Hey, Michelle was looking
good for you, tonight.

DON
Yes, she is beautiful; but
I told myself that I
wasn't messing with her
anymore. I can't be with
anyone's girl because I
know how it feels.

MALIK

Yeah. Hopefully she isn't, because I can tell that she is really into you.

(Malik says while getting into the car.)

She just stares at you how my wife stares at me.

DON

Alright man. Drive safe.

(Don saying while turning to go back inside.)

CHAD and TONY walks outside and head to the parking lot.

DON

Are you guys out?

CHAD

Yeah, man. We have to work in the morning.

TONY

Alright, Brother.

DON

Alright.

DON receives a text message and it's from MICHELLE.

MICHELLE

[Text]
Where are you?

DON

[Text]
Outside.

MICHELLE
[Text]
Okay. I'm coming out.

MICHELLE walks behind DON and puts her hands over his eyes. He laughs.

MICHELLE
Come walk to the car with me.

INT. ERICA'S CAR - NIGHT

DON
So how have you been?

MICHELLE
I'm okay. I started school for my Masters. I should have had it done by now, but I took off from school for the kids.

DON
That's great. You're doing it now, and that's all that matters.

MICHELLE
Yeah, you're right. I guess that I'm just ready to make more money. It's not easy trying to raise two kids.

MICHELLE stares out of the windshield.

MICHELLE

... and my kids are used to a certain lifestyle, so I have to keep working.

DON looked at MICHELLE and stayed quiet. Kids were a topic that he didn't know much about.

DON

I feel you.

MICHELLE

Let me stop being emotional. I had a great night. I missed your food for real.
... Oh! and you.
(Michelle smiled.)

DON

Contrary to popular belief, I kind of missed you to.

MICHELLE

Don't play with me. That's not popular belief.
(Michelle said laughing)

DON

You know that I missed you.
(Don said while hugging Michelle.)

MICHELLE looked at DON and blushed. She looked into his eyes and leaned over and kissed him. DON paused and leaned over and kissed her back.

MICHELLE
Let's go back in. I know Erica is waiting on me.

INT. DON'S APARTMENT. LIVING ROOM - NIGHT

DON and MICHELLE walked back inside of DON's apartment. ANGEL and JASMINE left; and ERICA fell asleep on the couch.

MICHELLE
This girl will fall asleep anywhere.
(Michelle laughs)

DON uses the restroom and walks into his bedroom. MICHELLE walks behind him and closes the door. She walks to the side of his bed and started undressing like she was in a rush.

DON
What are you doing?

MICHELLE
Stop it. You know what you want.
(Michelle aggressively says.)

DON took off his clothes and he and MICHELLE met with an aggressive kiss. MICHELLE bit his bottom lip and he grabbed the back of her head and pulled it back with her hair. He bit her neck as it stuck out from the bending. MICHELLE moaned in pleasure because she loved aggression. DON then slide his hand down to her neck and tightened before he threw her on the bed. MICHELLE opened her legs wide and welcomed DON in. He kissed her some more, then went for her breast. He pulled her breast out from the bottom of her bra and began sucking.

MICHELLE

I know they are small.

(Michelle insecurely laughed.)

DON

They are perfect.

(Don said with one in his mouth.)

Sit up.

DON tries to take off MICHELLE's bra, but couldn't seem to get it off.

DON

What kind of bra is this?

(Don laughed)

MICHELLE turned the back of her bra to the front and took it off. She threw it in the corner in urge and pulled DON back in. MICHELLE moved like she was in a rush for time. DON entered her and immediately pounded deep inside of her. MICHELLE screamed in pleasure.

DON

Shhhh!

(Don said while stroking)

MICHELLE

I'm Sorry.

(Michelle said while moaning)

DON continued to go deeper and deeper. Faster and faster. Spreading her legs wider and wider. Choking her harder and harder. MICHELLE screamed again.

MICHELLE

I'm sorry.

(Michelle said moaning.)

DON covered MICHELLE's mouth and it turned her on even more. He talked to her while he stroked.

DON
Didn't I tell you to be quiet.
(Don said while hitting a wall inside of her)
Huh? Huh?
(Don said every stroke.)

MICHELLE's response was muffled under his hand. MICHELLE tapped DON and got up. She turned around for him to enter her from behind. As soon and he entered her, she pushed back hard, throwing her body at him. He grabbed the back of her neck, pushing her head down into the pillow, and stood up inside of her. Every stroke was hard. After five minutes, MICHELLE tapped him again and turned to the side. DON entered her from the side while MICHELLE had one leg in the air. In this position, he focused on her ear, while squeezing her breast. He nibbled and licked all over her ear while whispering to her every stroke. He then began to blow in her ear, and MICHELLE jumped in pleasure.
MICHELLE changed positions quick again. It was like she was trying to experience every position in a short amount of time.

MICHELLE
Let me ride you.

DON turned over to his back. MICHELLE squatted and guiding him in. When the tip of his penis was in, she sat down. MICHELLE looked to the ceiling and moaned. She began to ride and moan some more. DON felt her getting wetter and wetter, and could tell that the climax was coming soon. When she was getting closer to climax, MICHELLE grabbed DON's hands and put them on her breast.

DON squeezed and MICHELLE moaned. MICHELLE's ride got slower and slower; harder and harder. She began to shake and fell on DON's chest. She laid there for two minutes, then immediately got up and went into the bathroom to wipe off. When MICHELLE came out, she found her clothes, put them on, and left DON in the room.

DON made a surprised look when she walked out of the room.

INT. DON'S APARTMENT. LIVING ROOM - NIGHT

MICHELLE
Erica wake up.
(Michelle said tapping Erica.)

ERICA opened her eyes and looked at MICHELLE.

MICHELLE
It's late. Come on.

DON walked into the living room as if nothing had happened.

MICHELLE
Thanks, for everything Don. We'll see you next time.

ERICA
Bye, Don.

DON
Bye.

DON silently walked them to their car, and sat until they pulled off.

SECOND OCTOBER

SECOND OCTOBER

DAY

SCENE

LOCATION

CAST

INT. COLUMBIA HIGH SCHOOL. MICHELLE'S OFFICE - MORNING

MICHELLE is in her office sitting at her desk, when she gets a knock on the door from a student.

[door knocks]

MICHELLE
Come in.

JAMES
Hey, Ms. Brown. Did you want to talk to me?

MICHELLE
Hi! How are you, James? You can sit down right there.
I just had a talk with your teachers.

MICHELLE pauses and stares at JAMES.

MICHELLE
... and they said that you've been doing great in class.

JAMES smiles.

MICHELLE
I'm happy to see that our talk was beneficial and you're back on track.
I know that it's been hard for you having to deal with your brother being gone, but you have to be strong for your mother. She already has to deal with your brother being locked away for a while, so it's up to you to keep her happy. In life, there are going to be many ups and downs, but you can't

let it stop you. This is your time to be stronger. Graduate, and be great, so that you can show your brother another way. You are a good kid James; with great potential. I don't want to see you mess that up. You were blessed to come to a school that many of the boys from your neighborhood dreamed of. Do you realize that?

JAMES

Yes, ma'am.

MICHELLE

I just want to say that I'm proud of you, and I'll continue to check up on you.
You can go back to class now.

JAMES

Okay. Thanks, Ms. Brown.

MICHELLE gets up and grabs the door for JAMES to let him out.

She goes back to her desk and stares at her boy's pictures on her desk with emotion.

INT. COLUMBIA HIGH SCHOOL. MICHELLE'S OFFICE - AFTERNOON

MICHELLE is on the phone with a parent, when a colleague comes to her office.

MICHELLE

[phone call]

Okay, Mrs. Douglass. I
just wanted to inform you.
Call me back if you have
any further questions.
Have a great afternoon.

MS. LINDA stands in the door way waiting on MICHELLE to finish her call.

MICHELLE

Hey, Ms. Linda.

MS. LINDA

Hey, Michelle. Are you
riding with me to lunch?

MICHELLE looks at her watch.

MICHELLE

Wow! It's time for lunch
already?
... and I'm hungry too.

MICHELLE grabs her purse, combs her hair, and walks into the hall with MS. LINDA.

INT. CAFE LE RU - AFTERNOON

MICHELLE and MS. LINDA is having lunch at a nearby café.

MICHELLE

I love this place. The seafood reminds me of home.

MS. LINDA

Yes. I love Creole. I got my Bachelors in Louisiana, and that's all we used to eat.

... but that was so long ago. You probably weren't born yet.

(Ms. Linda says sarcastically)

MICHELLE

Oh, Ms. Linda, stop it! I'm not that young.

... and you're not that old.

MS. LINDA

Well, you're making all of us feel old. Girl look at you. You're beautiful.

MICHELLE

Thank you. You are beautiful too.

MS. LINDA

I'm serious. All of the teachers talk about you. Even Principal Miller.
... and the students love you.
I guess that they connect with you more.
I setup a hair appointment for this weekend. I'm going to do something different with it. You motivated me to stay young and fresh. I kind of got lost living the boring life of a teacher.

A waitress comes in and breaks up the conversation.

WAITRESS

Is everything okay? How is the food?

MICHELLE

Everything is delicious. Thank You.
We would like the check please.

WAITRESS

No problem. I'll be right back.

INT. MICHELLE'S HOUSE - AFTERNON

MICHELLE walks into the house from work with the kids, when she notices that CHRIS is home early from work. She gets the kids settled, then finds CHRIS.

MICHELLE

Hey.

CHRIS

Hey.

MICHELLE

If I would've known that you didn't go to work today, I would have told you to pick up the kids.

CHRIS

I did go to work.

(Chris said in a low voice.)

... They suspended me today.

MICHELLE

Oh, Man! I'm sorry to hear that. What happened? Why would they feel the need to suspend you?

CHRIS

Well...I was late on a couple of projects.

MICHELLE

Late? That's unlike you.

CHRIS

I know. I haven't been myself lately.

MICHELLE

Well, you haven't been yourself in a while.
I guess that someone else sees it too.

CHRIS stays silent. MICHELLE walks away.

INT. DON'S APARTMENT - EVENING

DON is at home looking at some product photography on his computer, when he gets a call from MALIK.

DON

[answers call]

What's up, Malik?

MALIK

What's up.

I went to the car lot earlier today.

Have you talked to Amber lately?

DON

No. I haven't talked to her.

MALIK

Well, I think she is pregnant. She has a little pudge.

Did you use a condom? Do you think it could be yours?

DON

I doubt it. There is a possibility, but it was only once.

Hold on. Let me check her page.

She blocked me from looking at her page. I guess that she didn't want me to see her get bigger.

MALIK

Damn. That's crazy. Alright. I was just letting you know.

DON

Alright.

INT. MICHELLE'S HOUSE. LIVING ROOM - NIGHT

MICHELLE is laying on the couch in a t-shirt looking at the news.

NEWS REPORTER

We begin with the threat of a major hurricane making landfall on the East Coast. Tropical storm Assata, expected to strengthen as it moves toward the Carolinas. A state of emergency has already been declared by the governor of South Carolina.

MICHELLE turns off the television.

MICHELLE

All of this rain is making me sleepy.

(Michelle says to herself.)

MICHELLE gets up and walks upstairs.

INT. MICHELLE'S CAR - EVENING

MICHELLE is in her car driving when a tree falls into the road and hits the hood of her car.

[BOOM]

MICHELLE

Oh, My God!

(Michelle screams in panic.)

MICHELLE sits in shock, fear, and disbelief. Her eyes are dancing as she turns on her hazard lights. She then calls her insurance company and gets out to look at her car.

After calling the insurance company she calls CHRIS.

[phone rings]

CHRIS

Hello.

MICHELLE

Hey. I just got into a wreck. A tree came down and hit my hood when I was driving.

CHRIS

Oh, Man. Are you okay? Are the kids okay?

MICHELLE

Yes. I was driving by myself.
...going to pick something up for the kids. My mom has them. I've already called the insurance company. I'm just waiting on the tow truck to get here.

CHRIS

Does the car look totaled?

MICHELLE

No. The hood is messed up a little, but I don't think that it is totaled. ... hang on for a minute. My mom is calling on the other line.

BRENDA

Oh, My God! Baby are you okay?

[later]

EXT. ROAD - NIGHT

The TOW TRUCK DRIVER gives MICHELLE a copy of her tow receipt and hops in the truck. MICHELLE gets in the car with ERICA.

INT. ERICA'S CAR - NIGHT

MICHELLE

Girrrrlll!

(Michelle screams.)

I just don't know what to do. I don't know if I'm doing the right thing or not.

ERICA

Mmmm! That man got you driving through hurricanes to get to him.

(Erica laughs.)

My friend is officially gone. Did you talk to him?

MICHELLE

No. I'm so embarrassed. I don't even know what to do.

INT. DON'S APARTMENT - AFTERNOON

DON is at home when he receives a text from MICHELLE.

MICHELLE

[Text] [picture message]

Hey I'm sorry that I didn't text you last night. I got into a wreck on the way to your house.

DON

[Text]

That's okay. I'm sorry to hear that. Why didn't you call me?

MICHELLE

[Text]
I didn't want to bother
you with my problems.

DON

[Text]
It isn't about bothering
me. It's about making sure
that you are safe.

MICHELLE smiles at the phone.

MICHELLE

[Text]
Well now I know. Thanks.
I'm going to get a rental
car now. Maybe I can stop
by before I go back home.

DON

[Text]
I would love that.

INT. DIAMOND'S HOUSE - EVENING

MICHELLE is at her friend's house having a book club meeting. They are discussing the book and having drinks.

CHARISSE

Damn, that was good. Why can't I just find a man out of a book?

DIAMOND

Yes! I'm about to get out of this book club because I'm starting to get jealous.

BOOK CLUB WOMAN 1

It's just a book. This stuff isn't real.

MICHELLE

It's not that bad... Men like this do exist.

DIAMOND

Says the person with the perfect relationship. You need to find us a man.

MICHELLE

Girl, stop! No one's relationship is perfect. Excuse me ladies, I have to use the restroom.

INT. DIAMOND'S HOUSE. BATHROOM - EVENING

MICHELLE calls DON.

DON

Hello.

MICHELLE

Hey. How are you?
I was wondering if you still wanted me to come by.

[music and laughter in the background]

DON

I'm good. Of course I want you to come. Are you hungry?
I can wait on you before I eat.

MICHELLE

Yes. We have a few things here, but I'll wait to eat.

(Michelle says while throwing an appetizer in the bathroom trashcan)

[knocks on the door]

DIAMOND

Michelle!

(Diamond yells)

MICHELLE puts the phone to her chest.

MICHELLE

Yes!

DIAMOND

We are about to toast.
Girl hurry up.

MICHELLE

I'm coming. Hold on.
(Michelle yells.)
Hello.

DON

It's sounds like you're
having a good time.

MICHELLE

Yeah. Something like that.
I'm at my friend Diamond's
house. This is my other
friend. She likes to
party.

(Michelle laughs)

DON

I can see you now. I bet you're dancing. Probably off beat too.

(Don laughs)

MICHELLE

How do you know? You know me too well.

(Michelle laughs.)

I'll call you when I'm on the way.

DON

Okay. I'll leave the door open. Surprise me.

INT. DIAMOND'S HOUSE. LIVING ROOM - EVENING

All of the girls are in the living room dancing and singing.

BOOK CLUB

(The girls sing.)

Tonight I'm going to dancc for you!

INT. DIAMOND'S HOUSE - NIGHT

The girls are cleaning up and wrapping up the night.

BOOK CLUB WOMAN 2

Alright, ladies. That's it
for me.
I have to head home and
put the kids to bed.

MICHELLE

Yes. Me too.

DIAMOND

Okay, Girl. And Michelle
you can't leave yet.
You know that we barely
see you.

MICHELLE

Girl, I'm tired.

CHARISSE

I don't know Diamond. We
have been seeing Michelle
a lot lately.
(Charisse says
sarcastically.)

MICHELLE

A lot?

CHARISSE

I'm just saying.... But be safe going home girl. Love you.

MICHELLE

Love you too. Bye, Ladies.

INT. DON'S APARTMENT. LIVING ROOM

MICHELLE walks into DON'S apartment and it's dark. She tries to flip the light switch, but it doesn't come on.

MICHELLE

Don!

(Michelle yells)

DON walks behind her and gently hugs her from behind.

MICHELLE

[gasp of fear]

There you are. What happened to the lights?

DON

The power went out in this area a few hours ago.

I prepared dinner on the
grill though. Can you grab
the wine bottle out of the
freezer, along with two
glasses?

DON lit his fireplace and went to grab the food off of the grill. Michelle prepared the wine and set the dinner table.

DON

Smells so good!
(Don says holding a
container of meat.)
You can bring the glasses
over here. I want to sit
by the fire.

DON prepared the plates in the kitchen, then brought them back into the living room.

MICHELLE

So what did you cook?

DON

You'll see....
Close your eyes.

MICHELLE closed her eyes, while DON prepared her fork.

DON

Open your mouth.

DON put the fork in MICHELLE'S mouth.

MICHELLE

Mmm! Is that steak?

DON

Lamb.

MICHELLE

Oh, that's pretty good. And this salad looks pretty.

DON

Apple-Cranberry salad...with almonds and feta cheese.

MICHELLE

Mmm!

DON

Mmmmmmm!

(Don yelled)

MICHELLE

What?

DON

This wine is prepared beautifully.

(Don said sarcastically)

MICHELLE

(giggles)

Stop playing.

Are you trying to be funny Mr. Forbes?

DON

No, ma'am.

MICHELLE

I'll cook for you one day.

DON

I didn't mean it like that. It was a joke. No worries.

MICHELLE

Yeah. But I remember that you said that a woman hasn't cooked for you in a long time. I don't think it's that they don't want to cook for you. Maybe they are just scared to.

You cook really well.

DON

You know what.... I haven't thought about it like that. Maybe you're right, but I appreciate the thought more than anything.

[moment of silence]

DON

Honestly, all of this time I was thinking that they were just lazy.
Perspective is everything.
A relationship can feel one-sided at times. Like a man constantly has to give to a woman.
I hope that I'm saying that right.

MICHELLE

I understand... but you have to look at things from both sides. That is definitely not the case.
... But I'm still not cooking for you.

(Michelle giggles)

DON turns his head in shock and grabs MICHELLE playfully.

DON

Oh, you're going to cook for me!

MICHELLE

No, Sir!

(Michelle giggles)

DON hugs MICHELLE and kisses her forehead.

DON

Well, I guess that I'll be cooking every day.

MICHELLE picks up DON's plate.

DON

You don't have to wash them. Just sit them in the sink. I'll get it later.

MICHELLE sits the plates down and comes back into the living room. She then sits closer to DON.

MICHELLE

This fire feels good.

DON

Yes, it does. It's my first time lighting it. I was hoping that I didn't burn us up.

(Don laughs)

[moment of silence]

DON

I guess that we can't have it all.

MICHELLE

Have all of what?

DON

The things that we want in a partner. We have to compromise some things. Have you ever heard of the 80/20 rule? Maybe we only have 80 percent of what our partner needs. We'll have to compromise the rest. Figuring out what we

are willing to compromise
is the hard part.

MICHELLE stares into the air.

MICHELLE

Yeah. I guess that you're
right.
...Compromise.

DON

What is your type? What
qualities do you look for
in a husband? Honestly.

MICHELLE

Mmmm... Are you sure that
you want to know?

DON

Yes! You won't hurt my
feelings.

MICHELLE

I like tall men. So six
feet or taller. Muscular
build. Physically and
mentally health conscious.
Fashionable. He has to be
able to wear a nice suit,

and occasionally dress down in jeans and sneakers. He has to smell good. Hmmm... Is funny, supportive, a provider, and a protector. Is faithful and respectful. A master of sexual stimulation. He also has to be successful in his career.... and has to make more than me.

DON

Sounds good. I didn't know that successful was a type.

(Don laughs)

MICHELLE

(Michelle laughs)

Well it's my type. Now it's your turn. What's your type?

(Michelle anxiously breathes)

DON

I hate to answer this question, and most of the

time I act like I don't know....
This might sound cliché, but... You! You are my type.

MICHELLE blushes.

DON

I'm serious. From the way that you look. Your body type. Your hair. Everything. You are beautiful. I wouldn't change a thing. So physically I would choose you. Now the qualities.... That's a pretty long list. First, we have to have chemistry. I love chemistry and I think that it is what attracts two people. She has to be intelligent in order for us to talk on a certain level. She has to have a big heart. That way I can know that she would love me and most importantly love my kids with everything. She has to be spiritual and faithful. She has to be in-tune with her mental and emotional health, just like her physical health. She has to be beautiful to me. Diet is important. I'll cook everyday if I have to, but what we put in our body is important. She has to have some kind of economic knowledge because money is the cause of a number of divorce. She has to have style and love to laugh because humor will get us through bad days.

MICHELLE

Wow! It sounds like you know exactly what you want.

DON

I do.

DON stands up.

DON

I know that you have to leave soon,

but before you go; can we go on a date?

MICHELLE

A date? It's too late to go anywhere.

DON

Who said anything about going anywhere?

DON gets up and starts lighting all of the candles in the area. He goes into the kitchen and grabs a bag of popcorn and poured the kernels into a metal mixing bowl, along with coconut oil. He then wraps the bowl with aluminum foil, poked a few holes in the top, and heads to the patio.

MICHELLE

What are you up to Mr. Forbes?

DON

Come out here.

EXT. DON'S APARTMENT. PATIO - NIGHT

DON lit the gas grill and placed the bowl on top. He grabbed a pair of tongs and begins to shake the bowl.

DON

This is going to be the best popcorn that you have ever tasted.

MICHELLE

Oh, that's what you're making? You are something else. Where do you learn all of these things?

DON

When you grow up without things you learn to improvise.

(Don laughs)

But I don't own a microwave because convenience is going to be the death of us.

[popcorn popping]

MICHELLE

You are weird...
In a good way though.

DON

Yeah, I hear that a lot.
It's said that a woman's

top want from a man is security... and I know that money makes us feel secure. But security is deeper than that to me. It's knowing that no matter the economy, the weather, rather the power goes out, or anything else, that my family is going to eat.

MICHELLE looks into DON'S eyes.

[popcorn stops popping]

DON turned the grill off.

DON

Come on.

INT. DON'S APARTMENT - NIGHT

DON goes into the kitchen and places the bowl on a cutting board. He adds powdered sugar and chocolate covered peanuts. He goes back into the living room and opens up a laptop and plays a movie.

DON

Does this count as a movie date?

(laughs)

MICHELLE

I'll give you a pass tonight.

DON and MICHELLE watches the movie in front of the fire.

SECOND WINTER

SECOND WINTER

DAY

SCENE

LOCATION

CAST

EXT. GYM - NIGHT

MICHELLE walks out of the gym and heads home. She calls DON on the way.

[phone rings]

DON

Hello.

MICHELLE

Hey. I was just in the gym when you called. I'm heading home now.

DON

Don't get too fine. You already give me enough trouble.

(Don laughs)

MICHELLE

I'm just trying to maintain. That's all. I don't work out to gain or lose anything...But I do go a little harder on the squats.

(Michelle laughs)

MICHELLE gets in the car and drives away.

EXT. MICHELLE'S HOUSE. DRIVEWAY - NIGHT

MICHELLE is sitting in the car talking to DON.

DON

The kids must be sleep. I didn't hear them when you got home.

MICHELLE

That's because I haven't seen them yet.
They will be on me in a minute.

DON

Damn. So you still haven't gotten home?
How far is the gym?

MICHELLE

I'm home. I'm just sitting in the car.

DON

You've been sitting in the car this whole time?
Damn! I get it.

MICHELLE

No, you don't. I just know as soon as I get in the house they are going to want all of my attention. I just know my kids.

DON

Okay. Well, have a good night Ms. Lady. I'll talk to you another time. I don't want to hold you up.

MICHELLE

Okay.

(Michelle says in a disappointed voice)

INT. DON'S APARTMENT - DAY

DON and TONY are at DON'S apartment having casual conversation.

TONY

Me and Chad are thinking about going out tonight. I heard about a few parties. You might as well come out tonight.

DON

You know that I don't go out.

TONY

Well, you need to instead of being in the house all of the time.

DON

Well, I have fun in the house. Plus, Michelle is on the way in town.

(Don says smiling)

TONY

Well, bring her with you. I'm sure that she doesn't mind partying with the fellas.

DON gives TONY a look that says, "You've got to be kidding me."

TONY laughs in defeat.

TONY

What's going on with you and Michelle anyway? Are you trying to be with her?

DON

Well, I really don't know. We don't talk much about her life at home. I guess that I just have to trust that she knows what she is doing. I know we haven't had sex in a while. I actually told myself that I wasn't going to have sex with her anymore. I just enjoy her presence. We have some great, deep conversations.

TONY

Oh, Okay. You sound like you have it under control. I learned a lot from you. I learned not to give my whole heart out, because I've seen love make you do some crazy things. Me personally... I don't trust a lot of women. I told you not to trust Amber and you got mad at me, and look what happened. You were head over hills for her. I was just telling you that she

may look different, but
may be just like the rest
of these women.

DON

I feel you, but I still
don't think that she was
like the rest of these
women. She might have had
some flaws, but it's
definitely levels to them.
And I had my doubts, but
Malik told me that love
was a gamble. He said that
you won't gain anything by
trying not to lose.

TONY

I feel Malik...And that
was deep and all; but my
brother you are a high
risk gambler.

(Tony jokes)

DON

You damn right! If I die,
I die.

(Don laughs)

I like my love deep.

INT. DON'S APARTMENT - EVENING

MICHELLE walks in the front door with bags, while TONY is in the living room.

MICHELLE

Hey! How are you?

(Michelle politely says to Tony)

TONY

What's up sister?

(Tony says jokingly)

I was just telling Don that he needs to come out tonight. Tell him that he needs to get out of the house.

MICHELLE

No, he is fine staying in the house.

(Michelle laughs in seriousness)

I'm going out tonight too. Where are you all trying to go?

TONY

We haven't decided yet.

DON walks into the living room.

DON

There she is? Mmm mmm! So beautiful.
The real Beyoncé.

MICHELLE

Stop! You're making me nervous.
(Michelle says blushing)

MICHELLE walks into DON's room and puts her bags down. DON follows.

MICHELLE

You make me feel like a little girl when I see you. I get butterflies in my stomach.

DON

Hurry up and put those bags down and give me a hug.

DON hugs MICHELLE tight and kisses her on the forehead. MICHELLE closes her eyes in pleasure. They stay there for a moment then continue conversing. They walk back into the living room completely ignoring TONY. TONY stares at them in disbelief.

TONY

You both really like each other.

(Tony says surprised)

I'm about to head out. Let me know if you change your mind.

DON

Alright.

TONY walks himself out of the door.

DON grabbed a bag of chips out of MICHELLE'S hand.

DON

Stop eating this junk food. I cooked dinner already and I have a movie that I want you to see.

MICHELLE

I have to get dressed. I'm going out tonight. It's Charisse's birthday. I'll eat after I'm done.

DON stood there without saying anything.

MICHELLE

Why don't you go out with your friends?

DON

I'm good. Just call me when you leave. I'll get up.

INT. DON'S APARTMENT. BEDROOM - EARLY MORNING

DON wakes up and looks at the time on the clock, then checks his phone. The clock says 4:20 A.M. and he doesn't have any messages or calls from MICHELLE. He then calls MICHELLE.

[phone rings]

[Voicemail]
Hi! You've reached the voicemail of Michelle Brown.

DON hangs up and calls again.

INT. DON'S APARTMENT. BATHROOM - EARLY MORNING

DON walks into the bathroom with the phone to his ear.

[Voicemail]

Hi, you've reached...

DON hangs up the phone and sits on the toilet. He stares into the air for a moment and then calls again.

[phone rings]

DIAMOND

Hello.

DON

Where is Michelle?

(Don says in a demanding voice.)

DIAMOND

She's sleep.

DON

What do you mean, she's sleep? I'm waiting on her to come here. Well, go wake her up.

DIAMOND

She was drinking and she won't get up.

DON

What!?

Oh, Okay. Well, tell her
to stay sleep forever.

INT. DON'S APARTMENT. BEDROOM - MORNING

[phone rings]

DON

Yeah!

(Don says in a
strong tone)

MICHELLE

Hey... I heard that you
called last night.
I'm sorry. I got drunk.

DON cuts MICHELLE off.

DON

I can't believe you man.
Like I said, stay sleep.
Your things will be on the
porch, and I'm about to
leave; so don't knock.

DON hangs up. The phone rings again and DON declines the call.

EXT. DON'S APARTMENT - AFTERNOON

MICHELLE walks up to DON'S door with a sad face. She sees a bag on the porch and grabs it. She looks in it and sees her bag of chips inside of a plastic bag.

MICHELLE

Oh, you're being real petty today.

(Michelle says to herself)

MICHELLE knocks on the door.

DON opens the door and walks away.

INT. DON'S APARTMENT. LIVING ROOM - AFTERNOON

MICHELLE walks through the door.

DON

Your things are right there.

I didn't want to leave them outside.

MICHELLE

So you don't want to talk?

I swear that I blacked out last night.

Why don't you believe me?

DON

Man, you got me feeling like a female.

(Don screams)

I'm in here cooking dinner for you and sitting here waiting on you to come back; and you don't come home?

MICHELLE'S eyes lit up. DON realized what he had said and paused before he walked away.

INT. DON'S APARTMENT. LAUNDRY ROOM - AFTERNOON

DON walked into the laundry room and starting pulling clothes out of the dryer into a basket. MICHELLE walked in after him.

MICHELLE

Don!

Before MICHELLE could say anything else, DON choked her. He looked into her eyes and she looked back. DON began to passionately kiss MICHELLE. He stuck his hand in between her legs.

DON

This is my pussy.

MICHELLE silently stared at DON. DON pulled her off of the wall, and put her on top of the running washing machine. He kissed her again while the washing machine vibrated her whole body. With his tongue, he began to make love to her breast, while his finger played with the juices in her panties. MICHELLE reached down and grabbed his hard erection. She began pulling it as an invitation to come inside of her. DON pull his hand away and walked away for a moment. He came back into the laundry room naked with a condom on. He yanked MICHELLE off of the washing machine onto her feet. He then turned her around and smacked her bottom with a little force. DON helped MICHELLE take off her clothes and then entered her from behind. He immediately stroked her with aggression. He talked to her every couple of strokes and MICHELLE moaned in reply.

After fifteen minutes of aggressive sex, DON stopped.

DON

Damn!

(Don screamed)

Damn! Damn! Damn!

(Don repeated to himself)

DON walked out of the laundry room and into the bathroom. He took a quick birdbath and came back.

DON

I'm sorry. The condom broke.

I knew that it was feeling too good.

(Don jokes)

MICHELLE

Yeah, it was.

DON and MICHELLE goes into the bedroom and sit in awkwardness. Regardless of DON's attempt to joke, he showed that he didn't trust MICHELLE through his outburst. He showed himself too.

INT. MARY'S TOY STORE - AFTERNOON

DON and MALIK are walking through a toy store shopping. MALIK's son is picking out gifts for his birthday and DON is shopping for his niece and nephews.

A pregnant woman walks by with her kids, and DON looks at her, then turns away.

DON

If karma exist, then I'm paying for it right now. For what? I don't know; but I'm paying for something.

MALIK

Well, karma does exist, but there is good karma and bad karma.
Do you feel like you have bad karma?

DON

I don't know. I'm trying to think about whether I did someone wrong. It's just crazy how all three of my ex are pregnant at the same time. I'm getting closer and closer to thirty with no kids or commitment to anyone. Plus, I keep seeing pregnant women everywhere. It's like they are living the dream that they wanted for us, with someone else. I don't know if I'm doing the right thing by putting my goals first or just wasting time.

MALIK

It's just not your time to have kids. But you definitely have to get

serious with someone
before you are changing
pampers at fifty.
(Malik laughs)

MALIK looks at his son.

MALIK

Because I'm paying my dues
now.

MALIK and DON are done shopping so they head to the cash register.

CASHIER

How are you gentlemen? Did
you find everything that
you needed?

MALIK

How are you? Yes, we did.
We're trying to hurry up
and leave before I have to
spend some more money.
(Malik laughs)

DON gets a little closer and MALIK smirks because the cashier is pregnant.

INT. MALIK'S CAR. ABE LUXURY MOTORS - AFTERNOON

MALIK and DON pull up to ABE Luxury Motors.

MALIK

I have to run in here really quick.

DON

Alright. I'm going to stay in the car.

MALIK heads inside of the building. A few moments later AMBER walks pass MALIK's car and then goes inside of the building. DON stares at her, putting most of his focus on her stomach.

A few moments later MALIK gets back in the car.

MALIK

Yeah, man I had to get this spare key for my wife's truck. It's so clean. I might drive it more than her.

MALIK passes DON his phone and shows him a picture of the truck.

DON

Yeah. That's clean.

MALIK

Appreciate it.

[a moment of silence]

DON

How did Amber's stomach look to you?

MALIK

It looks back to normal to me.

DON

Yeah. That's what I said. I saw her walking in the building.

DON stares out of the window in thought as they ride home.

INT. DON'S APARTMENT - EVENING

DON is at home reading a book when he gets a text from AMBER.

AMBER

[text]

So do you hate me that
much that you had to stay
in the car?

DON

[text]

Hate is a strong word. Did
you do anything where I
should hate you?

AMBER

[text]

No. Just asking. How have
you been?

DON

[text]

I'm great and you?

AMBER

[text]

I'm good. Just a little
under the weather right
now. I have a cold.

DON

[text]

Make some chicken soup and
tea. Make sure that you
add lemon and honey to

your tea. The acid will help fight the cold and the honey will soothe your throat. Add ginger too.

AMBER

[text]
Sounds good, but who is going to make that? You must be coming to do it for me.

DON

[text]
I can.

AMBER

[text]
I'll be waiting.

DON

[text]
Give me an hour.

INT. AMBER'S APARTMENT - NIGHT

AMBER opens the door for DON. He has a bag of groceries. They speak, but their greeting is very nonchalant.

DON

What's up? Dr. Forbes here.

AMBER

Hey. Dr. Forbes.
(Amber giggles)

DON

I'm making this chicken soup from scratch so it's going to be a while.

AMBER

That's fine. I'll wait.

DON goes into the kitchen and prepares the soup and tea. He bakes a few chicken drumsticks and adds it to a pot of stock, then adds vegetables. When everything is prepared, DON brings it to AMBER on a tray.

DON

Be careful because it's hot.

AMBER

Aww! This looks so good. I hope it works.

DON

It always does. Make sure that you gargle salt three times a day. Salt kills bacteria.

DON and AMBER look at television in her living room while she finishes her soup.

AMBER

That's a beautiful wedding. I'm tired of going to weddings now. All of my line sisters are either married or engaged. I'm just waiting on my turn.

AMBER hands DON a wedding invitation.

AMBER

I have to go to this one next month. I should be in the gym so that I could fit into my dress. I brought it too small on purpose.

DON

You look fine to me. That's a nice size.

AMBER looks at DON and jokingly rolls her eyes.

AMBER

I want kids too. How many do you want?

DON

At least two. A boy and a girl.

AMBER

I want a boy. I'm going to name him Parker.

DON

Parker?

AMBER

Yes, Parker!

DON

How do I say this? That doesn't sound like a name that matches your ethnicity.

(Don laughs)

AMBER

Well at least he will be able to get a job.

DON

I guess so. But I want to name my son after me. I guess that I will just have to own my own company.

INT. AMBER'S APARTMENT. FRONT DOOR - NIGHT

AMBER walks DON to the front door to let him out. They hug before they part ways.

AMBER

Thanks again for the soup. I feel better already.

DON

No problem.

AMBER

Next time dinner is on me.

DON

Okay, I'll write that down. Bye.

AMBER shuts the door.

INT. NIPSEY'S FISH MARKET. DINNER TABLE - EVENING

AMBER and DON are having dinner at a casual fish market.

AMBER

Mmm. This looks good.
Yours look good too. Can I
taste it.

DON grabs his plate.

AMBER

Hold on. Let's pray first.

AMBER grabs DON's hand and prays.

AMBER

Amen.

DON

Amen.

AMBER

Now back to your fish.

(Amber laughs)

DON puts a portion of his food on a spoon and feeds AMBER.

AMBER

Mmm. That's so good. Let's
trade.

DON

(Don laughs)

No, ma'am.
I'm going to cook this.
This is how I get my recipes; by going out to dinner.
I just add my own touch to it.

DON and AMBER have finished dinner so they continue conversation over wine.

AMBER

So, how is your business going?
Are you bringing anymore women food?

DON

(Don laughs)

Everything is great... And I don't mix business with pleasure.

AMBER

I'm just joking. Me either. I couldn't entertain anyone that I work with.

DON

Yeah. That's never really been my thing. I like my space.

INT. AMBER'S CAR - NIGHT

AMBER is driving home while DON relaxes in the passenger seat.

DON

This was a pretty long ride. What made you choose a restaurant so far?

AMBER

I just like that place. I haven't eaten it in a while.

DON

Yes, it was pretty good. I thought you didn't listen to music in the car. You have a whole playlist. I didn't know that you liked rap music.

(Don laughs)

AMBER

Yes, I listen to all kinds of music. I was saying that I don't have a favorite artist.

[moments later]

DON

You know that I thought that you were pregnant.

AMBER stares at DON with a look of surprise.

AMBER

So are you saying that I was fat?

DON

No. Well, I thought that you've gained too much weight quickly.

AMBER

Oh. Well, no I wasn't.

INT. AMBER'S APARTMENT. BEDROOM - NIGHT

AMBER gets in the bed and pulls back the cover for DON to lay next to her. DON lays behind her and holds her from behind. DON immediately gets erect and rests his hard penis on AMBER's rear. AMBER turns around and kisses DON and it gets heated. After a few minutes, DON reaches and grabs a condom from out of his pants pockets.

AMBER

Oh. So were you planning on having sex?

DON

No. But anything can happen so you have to always be prepared to be safe.

AMBER and DON continue. They have sex and go to sleep.

INT. AMBER'S APARTMENT. KITCHEN - MORNING

DON walks into AMBER's kitchen to grab his left over food before he went home. He opens the fridge and sees a case of beer and steps back in shock.

DON

What the hell.

(Don whispers to himself)

DON looks in the bag and sees a receipt with the name JOHN on it. DON takes a picture of it. Grabs his food and leaves.

INT. DON'S APARTMENT - MORNING

DON receives a text from AMBER.

AMBER

[text]

Good Morning, Dr. Forbes.

DON looks at the message in anger and ignores it. He thinks for a while then sends a text back.

DON

[Text]

Good Morning. Whose beer is that in your fridge?

AMBER

[Text]

Mine.

DON

[Text]

I knew that you would lie. I saw the name on it and I can't believe it. I don't

know if I even know who
you are.

AMBER and DON exchange a few more text, but the story still stays the same.

EXT. DON'S APARTMENT - MORNING

DON is outside of his apartment walking around talking on the phone.

[phone rings]

MALIK

Hello.

DON

What's up Malik? Man I
spent the night at Amber's
place last night and when
I woke up I saw a case of
beer in the fridge.

MALIK

Damn.

DON

So that means that someone
is getting comfortable
over there and left them

because they plan on coming back.

MALIK

Most definitely.

DON

On top of that I saw the dudes name on a receipt. It was like it was meant for me to see. It was too perfect. And she never cooks so she never thinks about what's in her fridge.

MALIK

So do you think she has a man?

DON

No, it was the dude John from the car lot.

MALIK

Wow! Yeah! I can see that.

DON

I'm so mad. I just want to go up there and curse him

out. I hate these old dudes that try to brush up on these young girls. You're married. I feel like this man took my family away from me.

MALIK

Hold on now. You can't only blame him. She knew what she was doing too. It definitely works both ways.

DON

I just want to text her again and make her feel bad.

MALIK

One thing about women that mess with married men, they already justified everything in their head. There is nothing that you can do to change her mind. As much as it hurts you have to let it go.

DON

You're right. And I don't even know why I care so much. Maybe I just feel played.
Alright man, I'm going to let it go. I'll talk to you later.

MALIK

Alright.

INT. CHAD'S DRIVEWAY. DON'S CAR - NIGHT

DON just pulled up to CHAD's house, but he stays in the car. He stares into the air for a moment then he calls MICHELLE.

[phone rings]

MICHELLE

Hello.

DON

What's up? Are you busy?
(Don says in a low voice)

MICHELLE

Well, I was studying, but
I can talk for a little
while. What's up?

DON

I'm going through
something right now
and I need someone to talk
to.

MICHELLE

Okay. I'm listening.

DON

I don't know how to say
this but... Do you
remember the young lady
that I told you about?
Amber. I went to see her
last night and found out
that she is talking to a
guy. A guy that she was
around when we were
talking. It seems like it
was meant for me to see
it. I guess that I just
needed closure.

MICHELLE

I guess so. So why do you care? Did you have sex with her?

DON pauses before he speaks.

DON

No.

MICHELLE

Okay. Well then it isn't something that you should be sad over. Now that you have your closure, you can move on.

DON

Yeah. You're right.

(Don says in a low voice)

[moment of silence]

MICHELLE

I just can't believe that you chose her over me. I risked a lot of things for you. You don't know what it takes to come see you as often as I do.

DON

No, that's not the case.

(Don says under Michelle's rant)

MICHELLE

I can't believe you... But that's how you all do.

DON

Hold up. Who is you all? Now don't compare me to anyone. Judge me off of my actions; not what someone else did.

MICHELLE

I thought you were different.

DON

What do you want me to do while you're home with your family? Sit here lonely?

(Don yells)

MICHELLE gets quite in the realization of what DON said.

INT. MICHELLE'S HOUSE. BATHROOM - NIGHT

MICHELLE sits in a bubble bath relaxing.

NARRATOR

As much as we have the right to focus on our own self-interest, others have the same right. Who are we to stand in the way of what someone else considers as happiness? Who qualified anyone to stand in the way of ours? As much as we want the world to stop for us, it never has and never will. The world moves on its own time. Love constantly calls, temptations constantly burn, and loneliness constantly haunts. Who are we to not allow someone to be selfish with their happiness?

INT. DON'S APARTMENT - AFTERNOON

[phone rings]

DON

What's up?

CHAD

What's up? What happened to you last night? I thought that you were coming over.

DON

I came. I was parked in the driveway talking to Michelle. I told her about Amber.

CHAD

What do you mean you told her about Amber?

DON

I told her. We're always honest with one another. She's cool. We can talk about anything.

CHAD

No man. You are wrong. You weren't supposed to do that. There has to be a line.

DON

Yeah, you're right. I shouldn't have told her. Damn! I would have felt a type of way if the shoe was on the other foot.

CHAD

Yeah, man. You have to fix that.
... And quick.

SECOND SPRING

SECOND SPRING

DAY

SCENE

LOCATION

CAST

INT. LOFT - AFTERNOON

CHRIS has a meeting with a realtor to look at a loft that he is trying to move in. MICHELLE meets him to take a look at it too. The realtor is a beautiful young lady that looks the opposite of MICHELLE.
MICHELLE enters the loft while CHRIS and the REALTOR are talking.

KAYLA

Hi. I'm Kayla Belton of Belton Homes.

MICHELLE and KAYLA shakes hands.

MICHELLE

How are you? I'm Michelle.

KAYLA

Nice to meet you. We were just about to get started.

They walk through the home with the REALTOR.

KAYLA

... and here is your kitchen. Tall ceilings and bright lights. Spacious enough for dinner parties or business dinners. Here

is your beautiful island
for maximum cooking space.
Even though you'll be
alone, it's fit for a
holiday feast.

CHRIS

I love it. I'm torn
between this one and the
last one, but I love this
area.

KAYLA

Yes. This is a beautiful
area.

MICHELLE

It's nice, but where are
the kids going to sleep if
this is just an open area?

The REALTOR and MICHELLE both stare at CHRIS.

KAYLA

I'll put them a set of
beds in this area.

(Chris says pointing)

They'll be fine.

MICHELLE

Well, I guess that you have it under control. I have to make it to class. We'll talk about it later.

MICHELLE turns to the REALTOR for a handshake.

MICHELLE

It was nice meeting you.

KAYLA

My pleasure. It was nice meeting you as well.

INT. SUZANNE SHANK UNIVERSITY - EVENING

MICHELLE is in class.

PROFESSOR

Make sure that you guys start picking the topics for your thesis. I know that it seems like a long time before you'll have to turn it in, but trust me. It will come quicker than you know it. I'll see you all tomorrow.

MICHELLE walks down the hall to head home.

EXT. TRAIL - MORNING

DON, CHAD, TONY, and MALIK just got done running a trail. They gather at the end of the trail in conversation.

DON

[takes a few hard breathes]

A Malik. Do you have an extra bottle of water? I forgot to bring some.

TONY

I have one if he doesn't.

(Tony says holding up a bottle)

DON

(Don laughs)

I usually only drink spring water, but I guess that this will do. Thanks.

TONY

Yeah. Make sure that you don't forget the spring

water when you go in the
wilderness with Michelle.

(Tony laughs)

I can't believe that you
are actually about to go
zip lining. The things
that we do for women.

CHAD

Zip lining?

(Chad screams)

DON

Hey.

(Don shrugs)

She said that she likes
the outdoors so I want to
do that for her birthday.
She has been to Vegas,
L.A, and New York these
last couple of years, so I
have to compete with that.

TONY

I don't know about dying
for it though.

(Tony laughs)

EXT. SMOKY MOUNTAINS - AFTERNOON

MICHELLE

[screams]

MICHELLE slides down the zip line screaming and DON is there at the end of the line.

MICHELLE

Oh, my God! That was fun.

DON

It was okay.

(Don laughs)

I'm hungry now.

INT. BLACK RIDGE CABINS - SUNSET

[pan sizzling]

DON is cooking while MICHELLE is on the balcony taking pictures of the sunset.

[camera shutter clicks]

MICHELLE

This is beautiful. Don come here.

(Michelle screams)

DON walks in smoothly, despite MICHELLE'S screams.

DON

What do you see?

MICHELLE

Look! A family of bears.

DON

Yes. They are beautiful.
Get some good pictures...
And don't fall down there
because I don't want to
have to fight a bear.

(Don laughs)

MICHELLE

I'm not silly.

(Michelle laughs)

DON

Then again, I think that I
may have to die for you to
prove myself to you. I can
see you now.
That's right. Die for me.

(Don laughs)

MICHELLE

Hmm! Yep!

(Michelle smiles)

self·ish

DON goes back into the kitchen to finish cooking dinner.

INT. BLACK RIDGE CABINS - EVENING

MICHELLE and DON finishes dinner.

MICHELLE

Woo! That was good as usual Mr. Forbes.

DON

Why thank you, My Dear. I have something else for you.

DON gets up and goes into the kitchen and comes back with a bowl with a candle lit in it.

DON

Here you go.

MICHELLE

(Giggles)

Awww!

DON

Not your usual cake, but fit for a queen...

Who likes banana pudding.
Hold on.

DON runs back into the kitchen and grabs a bottle of champagne and two glasses.

DON

Let's make a toast.

MICHELLE raises her glass.

DON

Thank you God, for health. Continue to help us navigate on the road to wealth. Thank you for a beautiful year. And thank you, her mom, and dad, for making this beautiful queen.

(Don laughs)

MICHELLE and DON taps glasses, and MICHELLE blows out her candle.

INT. BLACK RIDGE CABINS - NIGHT

DON and MICHELLE are in the hot tub drinking champagne.

MICHELLE

I can sit here forever. If only we could live here without the worry of bills.

DON

Only if. That would be the life. But we will have to figure out how to keep the bears away from our garden. And they may try to eat the kids.

(Don laughs)

MICHELLE

No, my boys are tough. Those bears don't stand a chance.

(Michelle laughs)

I'm worried about my little girl though.

DON

What little girl?

MICHELLE

The little girl that I'm going to have next. If I

decide to have another one.

DON

What do you mean? I want more than one child.

MICHELLE

More than one? I'm not trying to push two more out.

DON

Well I don't have kids. That's what you have to deal with when you are with a man with no kids.

MICHELLE

I don't know about that Mr. Forbes.

(Michelle frowns)

My poor body. I'm trying to keep this figure.

SECOND SUMMER

SECOND SUMMER

DAY

SCENE

LOCATION

CAST

INT. DON'S APARTMENT - NIGHT

MICHELLE opens the door and walks into DON'S apartment.

MICHELLE

Hey.

DON

How are you.

DON hugs and kisses MICHELLE.

MICHELLE

I took a look at some houses today here. One was so beautiful. It wasn't in my price range right now, but I'll be ready next year when I graduate.

DON

So you want to live here now?

MICHELLE

Yes. I'm thinking about it. My kids need to be closer to their other family and there are some

great opportunities here
for me.

DON

Okay. That's great. What
do you want me to cook?

MICHELLE

Umm. I want to go out
tonight. I appreciate your
cooking, but we don't have
to eat in every night.
Let's go to dinner.

DON

Okay. I just didn't see
the purpose when I can
cook the same thing.

MICHELLE

I just want to get out,
that's all.

EXT. DOWNTOWN - NIGHT

MICHELLE and DON walks out of a restaurant and take a stroll downtown.

DON

Oh, I know why you wanted
to go out now.

MICHELLE

Why?

DON

Because you wanted to wear those new heels.

(Don jokes)

They are elegant. I must say.

MICHELLE

(Michelle laughs)

You may be right. I wasn't thinking about you huh?

DON

Sure wasn't.

MICHELLE

Do you think that I'm selfish?

(Michelle curiously asks)

DON

Yes.

MICHELLE opens her mouth in shock.

DON

I think that everyone is selfish in a way. I think that you wouldn't be alive if you didn't have a sense of selfishness. You wouldn't have the willpower that it takes to take care of yourself and maintain a healthy life. Life is about balance. It becomes problematic when you are too selfish. Water can help us and hurt us. Meaning, too much of anything can be toxic. So, yes. You are selfish; but it's up to you to figure out the balance.

MICHELLE doesn't say anything. She walks silent in thought.

THIRD OCTOBER

THIRD OCTOBER

DAY

SCENE

LOCATION

CAST

INT. BARRON REALTY - MORNING

DON has an appointment to look at a rental property. He goes to the realty office and picks up the key.

AGENT

Good Morning. How can I help you?

DON

Hi, my name is Don Forbes I have an appointment to view a property.

The AGENT looks at a list and grabs a clipboard then passes it to DON.

AGENT

Fill this out and read the requirements. The fico score requirements are here. The income requirements for this property is four times the month's rent... And you can't have any collections on your credit within the last five years.

INT. RENTAL PROPERTY - AFTERNOON

[key unlocks door]

DON walks into the property with his sister SIERRA.

SIERRA

This is nice.

(Sierra says in amazement)

DON and SIERRA walk around the house.

DON

A nice big kitchen for me to cook in.

SIERRA

Yes! Party over here.

[continue to walk]

SIERRA

Wow! There is a bathroom for every room in here. I think that there is five bathrooms.

DON

Yes. This place is huge. Michelle is thinking about

moving here when she
graduates.
The boys can have their
own room.

SIERRA
Well leave me a room too.
(Sierra laughs)

[continues to walk]

SIERRA
I'm going to check out the
back yard.
(Sierra yells)

INT. DON'S APARTMENT - NIGHT

DON is at home making some of his products when he gets a call from TONY.

DON
What's up?

TONY
What's up bro? Did you go
and look at the house
today?

DON

Yeah, man. It's huge. We are going to have a lot of fun in there.

TONY

I was talking to Sam today and he said that he was looking for a place. I told him to call you because you may have enough room for him.

DON

Oh okay. Nah man. My bachelor pad days are over. I'm not trying to have different women run through there.

TONY

Oh ok. I feel you. I was just letting you know.

INT. SEBI'S FARMERS MARKET - AFTERNOON

DON is grocery shopping and receives a call from Barron Realty.

[phone rings]

DON

Hello.

JULIA

Hi, am I speaking to Mr. Forbes?

DON

Yes, ma'am. How are you?

JULIA

I'm great Mr. Forbes. I wanted to talk to you about the rental property that you applied for. Everything looks great on your application. The only issue was that you have a collection showing up for Berkeley Apartments. Does that sound familiar?

DON

The complex does sound familiar, but I don't know why they would have something on my credit report.

JULIA

Well, give us a call when you get that squared away. Until then, we are unable to move forward.

DON

Okay. Thanks.

DON hangs up and makes a face of disappointment.

INT. RA SUSHI - EVENING

MICHELLE is at a restaurant table waiting. DON comes in and greets her.

DON

Hey, beautiful.

MICHELLE

Hey, handsome. How are you?

DON

I'm alright.

MICHELLE

How was your day?

DON

I'll let you go first. You may have had a better day than me.

MICHELLE

Well, everything is going good with school. I'm already in contact with a school to work at. I'm going to work there until I get my doctorate. And then I can enter private practice. That's my goal.

DON

That sounds great. As for me...
I took a look at a house. It was so beautiful and just a little bit higher for what I'm paying now. Everything was great. I had more than enough income for it, but they denied me because I had something on my credit from six years ago. I called and it was for something with the carpet, but I wasn't even staying

there. My name was still on the lease though. I tried to pay partial and they said that they wanted it in full. There is no way that I'm about to pay the full price when it will be off of my credit in a year.

MICHELLE

Awww.

DON passes MICHELLE his phone and shows her pictures.

MICHELLE

Yes. This is nice.

DON

The thing that makes me mad is that you couldn't have had anything on your credit in the last 5 years; And they still denied me. I think that they just didn't want me to stay in that area. It's like we have to be perfect out here. Everything says one hundred percent on time payments on my credit report.

MICHELLE

That's okay. I'll help you find something else.

EXT. RIVER WALK - NIGHT

DON and MICHELLE walks and talks along the river.

MICHELLE

Don, have you ever thought about going back to school? I know that you are into entrepreneurship, but I think that school will be a good thing for you. Then, you will always have something to fall back on.

DON

Yes, I dream of going back; but I need money now. Four years is a long time... And with the financial debt that school brings, I don't know.

MICHELLE

You can do it. I think that you're too smart to not have it documented. I think that it will open the doors for you for so many opportunities.

DON

I don't see many guys that look like me getting those corporate jobs. That's why I was always into entrepreneurship. I got tired of being denied opportunities.

MICHELLE

I go to school with plenty of guys that look like you.

DON

Who? Name one?

MICHELLE

John Michaels.

DON

Man! John doesn't look like me.

(Don laughs)

MICHELLE

You know what I'm saying. Stop playing.

MICHELLE playfully hits DON.

THIRD WINTER

THIRD WINTER

DAY

SCENE

LOCATION

CAST

INT. DON'S APARTMENT - AFTERNOON

DON is packing up his things in his apartment. He works until the sun goes down.

INT. DON'S APARTMENT - NIGHT

[door opens]

MICHELLE walks through the door.

MICHELLE

Wow! This place looks so different empty.

DON

Yeah.

MICHELLE

I'm going to cry. So many memories here.

DON

I left the couch to sleep on. I still have some time, but I just wanted to clear everything out.

MICHELLE looks around with a sad face.

INT. DON'S APARTMENT - MIDNIGHT

MICHELLE lays on DON's chest as they talk.

MICHELLE

It's crazy that even in this empty apartment... on this couch. I'm still at peace with you.

DON

Love is being satisfied in the middle of nothingness. I listen to a philosopher named Alan Watts; and he always talks about peace in the state of nothingness. How humans worry about the past and the future, while animals just enjoy the moment. It's like we are prisoners of our mental gifts.

MICHELLE

That's deep.

DON kisses MICHELLE's forehead.

DON

In a room full of nothingness, I'm still happy with you.

EXT. DON'S APARTMENT - MORNING

DON is preparing breakfast as MICHELLE walks out of the bathroom from taking a shower. She sits and watches as he prepares their plates.

MICHELLE

You know Don. I've been thinking.

(Michelle stutters a bit)

I think that I'm going to just stay where I live. I mean everything is convenient for me there. I also will have help with the boys while I finish school.

DON looks at MICHELLE with a surprised face.

DON

So when did you think of this?

MICHELLE

I was thinking about it for a while, but I just came to the conclusion.

DON

I can't believe this.

MICHELLE

You can't believe what?

DON

As soon as I tell you that I'm going to stay with my sister you come to this conclusion? It's only for a while. I just can't sign for another year here.

MICHELLE

It's not because of that... And I don't know what we are doing anyway. You never tell me how you really feel.

DON sits down in silence.

DON

As much as you want me to think from your shoes, I can't. I don't have kids. I can try to think from that perspective, but at this moment I don't know what it feels like to make decisions with my kids always in mind. I don't have to always make selfless decisions.

LAST FEBRUARY

LAST FEBRUARY

DAY

SCENE

LOCATION

CAST

INT. MARY FORBES' HOUSE - MORNING

DON and MICHELLE walks into his mother's house on Valentine's Day. She meets MICHELLE for the first time.

DON

Happy Valentine's Day.

DON hugs his mother.

DON

Mom, this is Michelle.

MOM

Nice to meet you.

MICHELLE

Hey. Nice to meet you too.

(Michelle says in a shy tone)

DON has breakfast with his MOM and MICHELLE. MICHELLE and MOM converse while DON cooks them breakfast. They have red velvet waffles, with whipped cream and strawberries.

DON

Alright, Ma. We have to get our day started.

DON hugs his mother.

MOM

Okay. Love you. Thanks for breakfast... And it was nice meeting you Michelle.

MICHELLE

Nice meeting you too.

INT. DON'S CAR - MORNING

DON is driving when he receives a text from his mother. He waits until he gets to a red light and reads the text.

MOM

[text]
I like her. She sits right with my spirit.

DON

My mom said that you sit right with her spirit. She must don't see the craziness that I see.

(Don laughs)

MICHELLE

That's right mom.

INT. BRICE HOTEL - AFTERNOON

DON and MICHELLE check into their hotel. They put their bags down and tour the site taking pictures.

DON

Mmm Mmm Mmm!

(Don says walking behind Michelle)

MICHELLE

Stop!

(Michelle says blushing)

DON

Let me take a picture of you to show you how you look.

MICHELLE poses and DON takes a few pictures.

MICHELLE

Let me see. Oh, I do look good.

... Take some more.

(Michelle laughs)

INT. BRICE HOTEL - EVENING

MICHELLE and DON goes into the hotel's restaurant and eat dinner. Afterwards, they head back to their room. DON goes into the bathroom with a suitcase. He unpacks a present, candles, and flowers, then goes back into the bedroom area.

MICHELLE walks in to her surprise and comes back to get DON to join her in the bathroom.

MICHELLE

Thank you.

MICHELLE kisses DON.

MICHELLE

I got something for you.
Wait here.

MICHELLE gets dressed and comes back dressed in lingerie. She sits on DON's lap facing him and begins to kiss him. DON grabs her bottom and squeezes it as she rocks back and forth, grinding him. After a few minutes, DON gets up.

DON

I got something for you
too.

DON grabs a box filled with his products. He makes a hot bath and places flower petals in it. He then hands MICHELLE a container that says, 'Bey'.

DON

I made this inspired by you.

MICHELLE smells inside of the container.

MICHELLE

This smells good. What does Bey mean?

DON

It's the title of a ruler in Kemet. It has many different meanings in different countries, but to me it means Queen.
... in which you are.

MICHELLE

Aww! Thanks.

DON

Turn around.

MICHELLE turns around and DON sits her back on his lap. He begins rubbing her back with 'Bey'. He grabs a feather and tickles her skin with it for a few minutes. Then he kisses MICHELLE's neck, while continuing to rub her back. He dips his hands into the bath water and washes the product off of his hands. Then places his hand on her vagina. He rubs her clit for a few minutes, then sticks his finger inside of her vagina. MICHELLE moans, and DON takes his finger out and tastes it.

DON

Baby you taste so good.
Let me taste some more.

DON picks MICHELLE up and puts her on the edge of the tub with her feet in the water. He takes his clothes off and gets inside of the water. He gets on his knees in the tub and puts his face in between MICHELLE's legs. He kisses her thighs and then kisses her panties. Next, he rips her panties in half and places his tongue on her clit. He begins to nibble and suck on her clit while she rubs his head.

DON

This pussy taste so good.

MICHELLE

[moaning]

DON slides MICHELLE into the water and lays her on top of him.

MICHELLE

Hold up! I want to taste you. Stand up.

DON stands up and MICHELLE begins licking and sucking.

DON

Damn!

After a few minutes, DON slides back down in the tub. MICHELLE gets on top of him and starts riding slow. DON digs deep inside of her.

MICHELLE

Yes!

DON stands MICHELLE up and bends her over the tub. He speeds the tempo of the sex up. He gets more aggressive and smacks her bottom from time to time. DON chokes her as well.

After the climax, they get out of the tub and head to the bedroom. MICHELLE lays on DON's chest until they fall asleep.

EXT. BRICE HOTEL - AFTERNOON

DON and MICHELLE are standing in front of the hotel waiting on valet.

DON

I was accepted into USC. I wanted to wait until I saw you in person to tell you.

MICHELLE

Wow! Congrats. I didn't know that you put in an application.

DON

Yes. I put it in back in October. It was a long process, but it was all worth it. I got some of my clients to write recommendation letters for me. I suppose to leave at the end of March to get ready for the semester. It's a big leap for me, but I've been waiting on this moment for a long time.

MICHELLE

Wow! I have so many emotions.
I'm surprised, shocked, and excited.
I'm happy for you though.

That was one of the places that I had on my list to move, but I don't know if I want to raise my boys in the city.

DON

I don't want to live in the city either. I just have to do what I have to at the moment.
I have to stay on campus for the first year so it's definitely going to be uncomfortable for me. It may be the discipline that I need though.

The VALET DRIVER drives up. DON and MICHELLE tips him and drive away.

EXT. KELSEY FORBES' HOUSE - EVENING

MICHELLE pulls up to DON's sister house.

MICHELLE

This feels weird. I always stay with you when I'm in town. It feels so different.

DON

It's weird for me too. I had to get used to sleeping alone. It's always hard for me to sleep without you.

MICHELLE

Aww! I didn't know that.

MICHELLE pushes the button to open her car trunk. She gets out and gets a gift out of the trunk and gives it to DON.

MICHELLE

For you, Mr. Forbes.

DON

Thanks, Ms. Brown.

DON and MICHELLE hug and DON walks into the house.

THIRD SPRING

THIRD SPRING

DAY

SCENE

LOCATION

CAST

EXT. LOS VEGAN MOBILE RESTAURANT. 7TH STREET - AFTERNOON

DON is getting lunch at a food truck in Los Angeles. He is dressed up for an interview.

FOOD TRUCK OWNER

Don!

(She calls for Don.)

DON walks up to the truck.

FOOD TRUCK OWNER

Vegetable Curry and one Cucumber Water.

DON

Yes, Ma'am. Thanks.

DON puts a tip into the truck's tip jar.

FOOD TRUCK OWNER

Thank you.

DON

No, thank you. Have a blessed day.

DON eats his food on a bench and stares at the city around him.

INT. 28TH & GRACE HEALTH AND BEAUTY - AFTERNOON

DON is in an interview with a health and beauty company.

INTERVIEWER

Well, nice to meet you Mr. Forbes. I look forward to talking to you soon. I think that you would do well as a brand manager for us.

DON

Thank you for the opportunity.

DON and the INTERVIEWER shakes hands.

EXT. LOS ANGELES - AFTERNOON

DON walks down the street talking to his mom.

DON

Yes. Everything went great. I love the company. The environment feels great; and the pay is awesome too. I'm just excited for this opportunity. I finally got

a chance to showcase my
skills.

MOM

That's great. I'm proud of
you, Son. The job is
already yours.

DON

Thanks. I know that I'm
going to kill it.
I'll talk to you later.
This is Dad on the other
line.

MOM

Okay. Love you.

DON

Love you too.

DON answers the other line.

DON

Hey, Pop.

[three weeks later]

INT. SHAWN LENARD LAW FIRM - AFTERNOON

DON walks into a law firm and meets a client.

SHAWN

Don. What's up man?

SHAWN is sitting at his desk. He stands up to greet DON.

DON

Everything is good. Here is your package. I hope that your wife loves it.

SHAWN

Thank you. It's our anniversary of nine years. I have a few things in store for her. This is going to make her day.

DON

Congratulations! And thank you for your business.

DON looks at a picture on SHAWN'S desk.

DON

I see that you have a big family.

SHAWN

Yeah, man. Five kids.

DON

Beautiful. I don't have any, but I think that I'm ready.

SHAWN

Take your time. I love my kids more than anything in the world, but it's definitely tough sometimes. I have the best wife in the world so that makes it easy for me. I know how hard that she works for the kids, so on weeks like this I have to make sure that it's really special for her.

DON

Most definitely.

I was dating this young lady for three years and I know that it's time to take things to the next level or let it go. She's everything that I want in a woman. I just want to

have everything in order
in my life before I commit
on that level.

SHAWN

Yes. I feel you. I don't
think that people fully
understand the title of a
husband. You have to be
the protector and provider
for your family through it
all.
My advice would be to own
a home and have a
comfortable amount of
income because kids aren't
cheap.
Most importantly, you have
to love her. Do you love
her?

[moment of silence]

DON

Yeah.

SHAWN

Are you sure? There was a
hesitation.

DON

No one has ever asked me that before. I think that I'm just realizing that myself.

SHAWN

Well, that's all you need. Good luck.

DON

Thanks man.

EXT. LOS ANGELES. MELROSE AVE - AFTERNOON

DON walks down Melrose Avenue holding a shopping bag. He sees a jewelry store and walks in.

INT. MILAN GALERIE - AFTERNOON

DON stares at wedding rings and glances at the high prices.

DON

Wow!

SALES WOMAN

Hi. That one is a one of one. We call it Queen Elizabeth.

DON

How are you? It's beautiful.

SALES WOMAN

What style ring does she like? We have emerald, princess, cushion, oval, pear, round, and marquise diamonds.
I'm a pear girl myself.
I have some more rings over here.

The SALES WOMAN walks to another part of the glass counter. DON follows.

DON

We never had that conversation. I'm trying to get an idea of what to buy.

SALES WOMAN

Okay. Tell me a little more about her.

EXT. PARKING GARAGE - SUNSET

DON sits in his car at the top of a parking garage. He sits in silence and then breathes in anxiety before he makes a call.

[phone rings]

MICHELLE

Hello.

DON

Hey. How are you?

MICHELLE

I'm good. Preparing dinner for the kids.
How are you? I haven't talked to you in a while.

DON

I'm great. Everything is lovely here. I meet so many interesting people from all over the country. My products are also doing pretty well here. I met this guy that brought a few things for his anniversary and we had a

conversation about
relationships. He told me
a few things about
marriage and kids; and I
thought about you.
When I mentioned your name
he asked me do I love you.
It was crazy because no
one ever asked me that
before.
I paused for a minute and
said, yes.

MICHELLE

Oh, wow. That's good to
know. I never knew that.

DON

We also talked about home
ownership and what it
takes to be a husband and
father. I think that I'm
ready. I have a little
anxiety, but I'm ready.

MICHELLE

Hold on Don! What are you
trying to say? Who said
anything about a
relationship? It's great
to know that you love me,

but I don't even know if I want that now. I just want to focus on my career and bettering myself.

DON

Yeah. You're right. I just thought that, that was what you wanted... that's all.

MICHELLE

Yes. That's what I wanted.

(Michelle says with emphasis)

DON sits in silence.

MICHELLE

Like I told you back then. I'll tell you again now. I love you too.

WOMEN IN PSYCHOLOGY EVENT

WIP
WOMEN IN PSYCHOLOGY

WOMEN IN PSYCHOLOGY EVENT

DAY

SCENE

LOCATION

CAST

[three years later]

INT. LAX AIRPORT - AFTERNOON

MICHELLE is walking with her bags when she is greeted by her car service driver.
He is holding a sign with her name on it.

WILLIAM
Hello. Are you Michelle Brown?

MICHELLE
Yes, I am... And you must be William.

WILLIAM
Yes. Nice to meet you Michelle. Welcome to Los Angeles.

MICHELLE
I'm happy to be here.

WILLIAM
Can I help you with your bags?

MICHELLE

Yes, you may. Such a gentleman. Thanks.

WILLIAM takes MICHELLE's bags and heads to the car.

INT. TRAFFIC - AFTERNOON

WILLIAM and MICHELLE are driving in traffic heading to her hotel.

WILLIAM

Your hotel is about an hour away.

MICHELLE

Okay. I have some emails to answer anyway. It's fine.

MICHELLE scrolls through her phone in the back seat.

WILLIAM

So, which event are you attending this weekend? I know that there are a couple.

MICHELLE

I'm speaking at the Women in Psychology event on tomorrow.

WILLIAM

Wow. Good luck.

MICHELLE

Thanks. I'm excited.

INT. THE RITZ-CARLTON LOS ANGELES. ROOM - AFTERNOON

MICHELLE unpacks her bags and hangs her clothes. Then she unpacks the gift box that DON gave her. It was a little worn, but was filled with new products. She set up the hotel bathroom with candles.

INT. UNIVERSITY OF SOUTHERN CALIFORNIA - MORNING

The Women in Psychology event kicks off. The building was filled with women. Some were at the vendor's tables, while others sat in preparation for the program. MICHELLE is backstage. A woman walks in the door.

WOMAN

Here she is sir.

The woman directed KEVIN to MICHELLE. KEVIN walked in with flowers and MICHELLE'S eyes lit up.

KEVIN

There she is.

KEVIN hugged MICHELLE.

KEVIN

Congratulations.

MICHELLE

Thank you, Honey. I'm glad to see that you made it.

MICHELLE kisses KEVIN.

MICHELLE

I'm about to get my makeup done.

KEVIN

Okay. I'm about to go find a seat.

MICHELLE sits in the makeup chair.

INT. UNIVERSITY OF SOUTHERN CALIFORNIA - AFTERNOON

The speakers gathered and were directed by the PROGRAM DIRECTOR.

PROGRAM DIRECTOR

Okay, ladies. We're going to take a few pictures and then we have an interview room setup for questions before we get started.

The ladies went onto a red carpet and posed for pictures. Afterwards they walked into the interview room.

JOURNALIST

How are you Ms. Brown? We hear about a range of topics that are going to be discussed this evening. What are you planning to cover?

MICHELLE talked to all of the journalist in the room. In the middle of an interview DON walked in.
MICHELLE looked at DON and froze.

MICHELLE

Damn.

(Michelle said to herself)

MICHELLE continued with her interview.

MICHELLE

Well, I think that the industry is going in the right direction. We are also bringing more awareness to mental health in our communities.

DON glances at MICHELLE in surprise, and greets the camera crew.

[moments later]

The PROGRAM DIRECTOR gives the ladies a quick lesson on the wireless microphones and then the camera crew helps the ladies hook them up to their outfits.
DON gives MICHELLE her microphone.

DON

Here you are Ms. Brown.

MICHELLE

Thank you.

[moment of silence]

DON

You'll just strap this wherever you feel

comfortable... and put
this behind your ear.

MICHELLE

What are you doing here?

(Michelle whispers)

DON

Working. How are you?

MICHELLE

I'm good. Just surprised
to see you.

DON

I don't know whether
that's a good or bad
thing.

MICHELLE

Yeah. Me either.

DON

Good luck on your speech.
I know that you'll kill
it.

MICHELLE

Thanks.

Are you apart of the production crew?

DON

Yes. We're doing all of the production for the weekend. So I'll be around all weekend.

[moments later]

The MODERATOR introduces MICHELLE.

[crowd applause]

MICHELLE

[speech]

As a woman. And as a woman in psychology, I'm expected to absorb the problems of the world. My super power is taking the world's negative energy and giving that energy back to the world in a new positive form. With great power comes great responsibility. With great responsibility comes a strict commitment. So I've committed every day to keeping the world calm. I wake up and pour into the world. Wake up and pour into the world. Wake up again, and pour into the world. A process that I love... but... Then I come back home with an empty cup. So I have to refill, and repeat again. Super woman! We are super women in psychology. But what happens when the world has drained out all of our power? How do we recharge? We know how to pour into the world, but have we forgotten about ourselves? Are we allowed to put our pitcher down and pull out our glass? Are we allowed to be selfish? I want to challenge what we think about the word selfish. I want to change the way that we think about caring for self. As we know it today, the word selfish means being devoted to or caring only for oneself. In other words, committed to self-care. So if the definition only means this, where did the word go wrong? Being selfless, self.... less, is defined alongside words like noble, charitable, and generous; while self-interest is looked down upon. We can be self-interested without the expense of hurting others. If indeed we change the world by changing ourselves, then it is productive to the world to be selfish.

If we are constantly meeting the demands of the world, are we satisfying ourselves? I agree that as a society it is more beneficial to the majority for everyone to work together; but the world also works on balance. I want everyone to go out into the world and uplift it, but I also want everyone to put that same amount of energy into themselves. Our place that we call home should be a place where we can be selfish. A place that we can have full peace and not worry about the politics of the world. A place that we are held to our own standard and not the standard that the world has set for us.

[time passes]

MICHELLE

Ladies, you are beautiful. You are strong. You are intelligent; and you are committed. You are the foundation of the world, and everything enters through you. You are the nurturers. You are the healers. You are the teachers. Your job is much greater than your career in psychology. You are magic. While letting the world borrow some of your magic, don't forget about healing, nurturing, teaching, and providing for yourselves. Thank you.

[crowd applause] [crowd cheers]

INT. LAX AIRPORT. RESTAURANT - DAY

MICHELLE is at a restaurant reading a brochure that says 'Research in Child Development'. Her smart watch's alarm beeps and has a reminder that says 'FLIGHT'. MICHELLE waves for her waiter and rushes to her flight.

INT. PLANE - DAY

The plane is getting ready for takeoff. The Airline's safety video is playing.

[safety video]
If you have a carry-on, please place it under the seat in front of you. If it won't fit under your seat, please place it in the overhead bin.

MICHELLE pulls out a laptop from her bag and places her luggage under the seat. She opens a file on her laptop that says 'Women in Psychology Speech'.

[safety video]

If you have a hand held device, please switch it to airplane mode.

MICHELLE opens her phone and she is flooded with emails, text, and missed calls. She responds to only one text then puts her phone on airplane mode.

MICHELLE

[Text] [To Chris]

We're departing now.

[safety video]

In the event that cabin pressure changes, the panels above your seat will open, releasing an oxygen mask. Place the mask over your nose and mouth, pull the elastic strap over your head, and adjust the mask if necessary. Breathing normally, will start the oxygen flow.

MICHELLE plays an album from her media player, puts on her headphones, and closes her eyes.

[safety video's audio]

Be sure to adjust your own mask before helping others.

EXT. CHRIS'S LOFT - NIGHT

MICHELLE arrives at CHRIS's loft to pick up the boys. CHRIS brings them out and they head home.

[two weeks later]

CLOSURE

CLOSURE

DAY

SCENE

LOCATION

CAST

INT. DR. MICHELLE BROWN'S WELLNESS AND THERAPY - MORNING

MICHELLE walks into her office and is greeted by her assistant.

MARIA

Good Morning, Dr. Brown.

MICHELLE

Good Morning, Maria. It smells so good in here.

MARIA

I made some fresh coffee with those Kenyan coffee beans that you ordered.

MICHELLE

Thanks. I'll try some of that now.

MICHELLE walks into the kitchen.

MARIA

You have three clients for today. Mr. and Mrs. Rodriguez, Ms. Davidson, and a new client. Mr. Don Forbes.

MICHELLE spills her coffee cup over.

MICHELLE

Oh, my God.

MICHELLE looks at the mess and begins to clean. MARIA grabs a mop and starts to help.

MICHELLE

That's okay. I got it. When did we set up an appointment for Mr. Forbes?

MARIA

Last week.

MICHELLE

Okay. It must have slipped my mind. What time is his appointment?

MARIA

1 P.M.

MICHELLE

Okay. Call him and cancel.

MARIA

Are you sure? You never
canceled an appointment
Dr. Brown.

MICHELLE stares into the air.

MICHELLE

I had a long evening
yesterday, that's all.

MARIA

Okay.

MARIA walks to her desk to call and email DON.

[4 hours later]

MICHELLE is finishing up a couple's therapy session.

INT. DR. MICHELLE BROWN'S WELLNESS AND THERAPY - AFTERNOON

DON walks into the building and MARIA greets him.

MARIA

How are you, sir? How may
I help you?

DON

Good Afternoon. I'm here for an appointment with Dr. Michelle Brown. The appointment is for Don Forbes.

MARIA

Yes, sir I see that you had an appointment for 1. I called you to reschedule. Dr. Brown is not open for that time.

[door opens]

DON and MARIA turn their head towards the sound and MICHELLE walks out with her clients.

MICHELLE

You all have a great evening.

MICHELLE walks her clients to the door and then turns around and greets DON.

MICHELLE

How are you, Sir?

MICHELLE gives DON a hand shake.

MARIA

Mr. Don Forbes is here for an appointment, but I just informed him that you were booked for the rest of the day.

MICHELLE

That’s Okay. I’ll take him.
Mr. Forbes, sign in and follow me.

DON signs in and follows MICHELLE to her therapy office.

When DON walks in, MICHELLE closes the door.

DON

Can I used the restroom before we start?

MICHELLE

Sure. It’s to your left.

DON walks into the restroom and is amazed by its design. He has never been in MICHELLE’s space before, so he was impressed. DON used the restroom and washed his hands. He was amazed by the rocks inside of her sink, symbolizing the ocean. Everything was peaceful.
DON walks back into MICHELLE’s office and takes a seat.

DON

This is a beautiful place.
And I love the paintings
by T.B. Douglass. Her art
is so calming. It's a
perfect style for the
peace of this office.
I'm very proud of you.

MICHELLE

Thanks, Mr. Forbes.

MICHELLE hands DON a clipboard.

MICHELLE

Before we start, I'll have
you read over these
documents and sign them.

DON signs each document without reading, and hands the clipboard back to MICHELLE.
MICHELLE places the paperwork into a folder and then sits it in her therapy chair across from DON.

MICHELLE

The session is starting
now. So Mr. Forbes, do you
want to tell me what
brought you in today?

DON stares into MICHELLE's eyes with focus before he speaks.

DON

I was at a powerful event about two weeks ago. With a room full of powerful women. One woman spoke about the idea of selfishness and it was like she was speaking to what I was going through at the moment. It was like she was in my thoughts; and it really resonated with me. It was sort of if a higher power orchestrated these words and placed me there to listen. I've been on this selfish journey for a while and accomplished many things because of it; but I know that isolation is like fasting. It's only productive for a certain amount of time before it becomes unhealthy. I know what's next, but the next part is what scares me.

[pause]

DON

After selfishness or independence, comes unity. Unity scares me. I'm obsessed with the idea of having a union, but I'm scared of failing at it. I'm scared of the dream that I've dreamed of my whole life becoming a nightmare. I guess waiting allows me to live in this dream a little while longer.

I understand the laws of life and the order that things are supposed to happen. It's crazy how time is the only thing that gives us the answer to what we are going through in the moment. So now I understand why I had to go through this period of selfishness.

I feel as if I had to go through this period in order to become the man that I've dreamed of being. I'm spiritually, mentally, and intellectually at my greatest level. I'm more focused and productive than I've ever been. Most importantly I'm happy and at true peace. I'm happy because I'm happy with myself. Everything that I'm doing now, I could have been doing, but I've never put this much focus into myself. I've always had external things around me that took my focus; including people. Because most people only get to experience our external self, we tend to spend more time with this version. I reversed my energy.

I moved away from my hometown about three years ago to go on a journey. I went on a journey to find myself and live in my true potential. I've always knew my worth, but I never knew if I would live up to the man that I had inside of me. I felt as if not walking in my true purpose was beginning to hurt my love life. The strong women that I'm attracted to are also attracted to a strong man, and I have to be that on every level. I feel like I've mastered many things in relationships, but security has always been a gamble for me. In entrepreneurship, you either can win big, or lose it all. I am willing to bet everything on myself, but I don't know if I can expect someone else to feel the same. When I moved, I knew that I was going to be starting my life over. Most importantly I had to build my business over in a new city and didn't know what the future would bring. With my pride, I knew that I couldn't let the woman that I've been involved with see any weakness in me. They say that a man finds out a lot about a woman when he has nothing, but my pride wasn't willing to take that gamble. Nights I prayed that I could just walk into quick success and send her the keys to a new house; but life doesn't work like that. For the first year, I was looking for great jobs, until I realized that I was only applying for jobs that other people would be impressed with. I didn't want any of those jobs, I just wanted to please everyone around me. One day, I just let everything go. It was hard to let go of love. It took the whole year to fully detox, but when I did, I started to progress. In the moment of love, it's hard to tell your partner your weakness, because we always want to be looked at in a positive light. This woman was so beautiful to me and I was kind of a prisoner to her opinion. I didn't want her to look at me any less than a King. When I let go of love, I was able to stand in my truth and make the proper adjustments. The second year was a rebirth. When we are born again, our mind is transformed. I changed my thoughts and put all of my energy into myself. I changed my life from the inside out, by changing my diet as well. I rebranded my business and invested in video production; in which I've always had a passion for. Plus, I've always did my own marketing for my products. Letting go of the past allowed me to make this change. The world teaches us to attach ourselves to something in order to be great, so I was looking to attach myself to a career. When we do this, we often let other people or a position define who we are. When we lose this position, we feel like we've lost ourselves. When I let other people define who I was, it made me depressed. I realized that people often only love you for who they want you to be. For some people, who the world wants us to be is so far away from who we are. Some can change themselves and live with the it, but I wasn't willing. After getting denied from opportunities that I'm certain that I was overqualified for; I knew that there was nothing that I could do to be accepted in a world that didn't want me. Apart of our unhappiness is trying to be a part of communities and cultures that don't accept us. We use other people as our measuring stick for success. As many people that there are in the world, someone relates to us. I stopped chasing and learned to attract.

The third year I started seeing progression. The seeds that I had planted had begun to grow and provide me with a new life. I started meeting knew people of like minds. People that was on the same path that I was on. This is the year that I became a master of my craft. My work became effortless, and with mastery comes success. One of the things that gave me the time to put in the mastery hours was isolation. Isolation was tough, but it allowed me to take a deep dig into myself. It allowed me time to get to know myself again. I think that isolation was so necessary, because it made me stronger.

I learned to adapt to being on my own. I had to depend on myself for everything; even my mental health. I had no one to call and give my problems to. I had to talk myself out of every problem. Now I'm able to control my own emotions and lift myself up. I don't have to look for happiness in a partner. I know that happiness is not my partner's obligation. My partner is committed to the union.

Another thing that I've embraced in the third year was celibacy. Today I'm two and a half years' celibate. It's one of the best things that I've ever done. It was unintentional, but after a while I accepted it. When I moved, my sexual trust level went down. With so many diseases in the world, it felt good not having to worry about that for a while. This was another thing that allowed me to have full peace. Also, I wasn't constantly taking in someone's energy. I got tired of the attachment that sex brings. It becomes hard to let people go that we are sexually attached too. I knew that it was time for me to find a wife, so I couldn't keep wasting years carrying sex partners through time. Now I'm firm about waiting for the right partner. I'm strict about who I allow in my presence.

A new city allowed me to look at dating different also. Every city has their own culture and things that attract them, so I had to learn new ways to attract women. What was successful back home, wasn't necessarily successful there. I noticed that the trust level was also different with women there. I found myself having to prove that I am trustworthy more than I would have liked to. I understood that it was only because the men that they were used to were untrustworthy. Over the last couple of years, I've watched women become empowered and thrive in business. With this being the case, the majority of my clients were women. As I built a stronger relationship with women, I started to listen to their feelings more. I learned about the things that bothered them and about the things that they've wanted. This made me look into the mirror and change a lot about myself. For the first time in my life I started listening to women, without feeling like I'm being punished.

Listening made me a better man and strengthened my communication skills. Now in my next relationship I can be comfortable in conversation instead of running from them in argument.

I got closer to the woman over these years and I watched her journey also. I watched her strive and achieve. I watched her fight for power and walk into power. I let her pour out all of her feelings and even let her confront me. I watched her at war for her rights and I sat back a listened. Now I just want us to have peace. I want to take my rightful place as King in her life. I want to tell her that she doesn't have to fight anymore. I want to tell her that she can love again.

In eliminating sexual pleasure, I found out that I find pleasure in many other things. I found out that pleasure isn't just limited to romance. I find so much pleasure in conversation now because I know how it feels to sit years in silence. Finding someone that understands our soul is a great level of pleasure. I just want someone to understands my soul.

After DON finish speaking, there is an awkward moment of silence.

DON breaks the ice.

DON

I know that, that was long, but thank you for listening.

MICHELLE

No, it was perfect.

INT. DR. MICHELLE BROWN'S WELLNESS AND THERAPY - AFTERNOON

MICHELLE walks DON to the door.

MICHELLE

Thank you, Mr. Forbes.
Have a great day.

DON

No... Thank you, Ms.
Brown.

MICHELLE closes the door behind DON and sits there in silence as her eyes water. She takes a deep breath then sits down at a chair by the door.
After a few minutes, her phone rings.

[phone rings]

MICHELLE looks down at her phone and it's a call from KEVIN.

PARIS

PARIS

DAY

SCENE

LOCATION

CAST

INT. EMMA DUPREE MEDICAL CENTER. ROOM - EVENING

MICHELLE is standing over KEVIN'S daughter hospital bed. KEVIN is standing behind her.

MICHELLE

Okay, doll. I have to leave. I'll see you when I get back. I hope that you feel better.

MICHELLE grabs KEVIN'S daughter hand.

PAIGE

Bye, Ms. Michelle!

MICHELLE and KEVIN walk to the door. MICHELLE stops and KEVIN kisses her.

KEVIN

Okay, Honey call me when you get in. I'll be here all night. I'm sorry that I can't make Paris. I'll make it up to you.

MICHELLE

Don't be sorry. This is far more important. I

would want you to stop the world for me too.

KEVIN kisses MICHELLE again.

KEVIN

See, that's why I love you. You understand.

INT. PLAZA ATHÉNÉE PALACE. ELEVATOR - AFTERNOON

MICHELLE and MS. LINDA is on an elevator going to their rooms.

MS. LINDA

This is such a beautiful place and that harp sounds so beautiful down stairs. It's so welcoming. Girl, thank you for bringing an old gal with you.

MICHELLE

Oh, don't mention it Ms. Linda. You are doing me a favor. I'm not bold enough to come here alone. I needed this though.

MS. LINDA

Me too. I've always wanted to come here since a little girl. Now I didn't think that it would take this long, but I'm here.

MICHELLE

(laughs)

You know me and a guy had an argument about this a couple years ago. Well, I guess that I had an argument by myself. I said that I'm getting married and having my honey moon in Paris by thirty. He said that he isn't going to argue with me about the future...Now that I think about it, it's funny that life never turns out how we imagined it.

The elevators open and the girls walk out.

MS. LINDA

It does sometimes. It just doesn't happen as fast as we like it. Life is a journey. We put so much

pressure on ourselves with
these time limits.
You are here though.

MICHELLE

Yes!
We are here.

MICHELLE stops.

MICHELLE

So, since we're going to be here for a week, I've decided that I'm staying in for my birthday. I want to spend some time to myself, and I think that you should do the same.

MS. LINDA

Agreed. Happy Birthday young lady.

MS. LINDA kisses MICHELLE on the cheek.

MS. LINDA

I'm very proud of the woman that you've become.
Love you.

MICHELLE

Awww! Thanks. Love you too.

INT. PLAZA ATHÉNÉE PALACE. ROOM - EVENING

MICHELLE walks around her room in a robe with a glass of champagne in her hand. Music is playing while she sets up a bubble bath.

[music playing]
[Ella Fitzgerald & Louis Armstrong- April in Paris]

[door knock]

MICHELLE opens the door to flowers and a birthday cake.

ROOM SERVICE

Pour vous, Mademoiselle.

MICHELLE

Merci, monsieur.

MICHELLE closes the door.

INT. PLAZA ATHÉNÉE. BATHROOM - EVENING

MICHELLE soaks in a soaking tub with candles all around her. Her cake's candle is lit, as she stares at it drinking champagne.

EXT. PLAZA ATHÉNÉE PALACE. ROOM BALCONY - NIGHT

MICHELLE sits on the balcony with her laptop, writing and email. She finishes it and hesitates to press send.

MICHELLE stares at the computer after she finishes it. The email is addressed to DON.

After a moment MICHELLE sends the email.

[one week later]

INT. CHARLES DE GAULLE AIRPORT - AFTERNOON

MICHELLE and MS. LINDA run through the airport to their plane.

Camera Fade-away

[background commentary]

[safety video's audio]
Be sure to adjust your own mask before helping others.

[CREDITS ROLL]

[MUSIC][Nina Simone- Isn't it a Pity]

CREDITS

DON FORBES
MICHELLE BROWN
AMBER MONROE
CHRIS
MESSIAH
AIDEN
CHAD
TONY
MALIK WILLIAMS
ERICA
DIAMOND
CHARISSE
SIERRA FORBES
MARY FORBES
KELSEY FORBES
BRENDA BROWN
JOHN HINES
JASMINE
ANGEL
MS. LINDA
JAMES
KAYLA BELTON
JULIA BARRON
MARIA
KEVIN
PAIGE
JOSH
WILLIAM
SHAWN LENARD

WRITTEN AND DIRECTED BY
DUSHAWN BANKS

POST CREDITS

POST CREDITS

DAY

SCENE

LOCATION

CAST

INT. PRODUCTION STUDIO - MORNING

DON is directing a morning Show. He directs the ladies.

DON

How are you ladies? Here are your microphones. You can go ahead and strap them on. We'll be ready to roll in about thirty minutes.

The ladies thank DON and he takes a break.

INT. PRODUCTION STUDIO. KITCHEN - MORNING

DON is at a table drinking a cup of coffee and reading a book when a young lady comes and talks to him.

ALICIA

Hey, what book are you reading?

DON

Hi. It's a self-help book called Selfish Sundays. It's written by a hundred-year-old woman. I use to buy natural products from her.

ALICIA

Oh, okay. I don't see many men reading books like that. That's interesting.

DON

Well, I'm not like many men I guess. We are lost when we don't have an overstanding of self. I'm all about knowledge of self.

ALICIA

Right. I was just saying that the other day. So where can I get a copy. It seems like something that I'll be interested in.

DON

I can order a copy for you as a gift from me.

ALICIA

Wow. Thanks.

I'm Alicia by the way. I've saw you on set, but we've never officially met.

DON

Hi, Alicia. I'm Don.

ALICIA pulls out a pen and writes on a napkin.

ALICIA

Here is my number. Maybe we can meet up when the book arrives.

DON looks down at the napkin for a moment, then he grabs it and places it in his book.

DON

That will work.

ALICIA

Well, thank you, Mr. Don. I'll talk to you later.

ALICIA gets up and walks away.

EXT. TRAINER'S HEAVEN - AFTERNOON

DON stood outside of the gym with a book in his hand waiting on ALICIA. ALICIA pulls into the parking lot and meets DON.

ALICIA

Good Afternoon.

DON

Good Afternoon. How are you?

DON shakes ALICIA's hand then gives her the book.

DON

For you, ma'am.

ALICIA

Thank you so much. I'm going to read this tonight.

I love this gym. I didn't know that you worked out here. I've been going here since it opened.

DON

Yes, this is a beautiful gym. I just started going here. I've been slacking for a while, but now it's time for my body to reflect the discipline that my mind has right now.

ALICIA

Well, from what I can see,
you look pretty
disciplined.

DON smiled.

DON

You as well.

ALICIA blushes.

ALICIA

Well I try.

Since I'm over here, I can
catch my favorite
restaurant. Do you have
time for lunch?

DON looks at his watch.

DON

Ughhh! Why not? I need
some post work out protein
anyway.

ALICIA

Yay! I'll meet you over there if you want to go and put your bag down.

DON

Okay.

EXT. VALET - AFTERNOON

DON and ALICIA stands outside of the restaurant waiting for their cars.

ALICIA

So, Don. What's a man like you doing single? Do you not want a girlfriend?

DON

No.

I'm past the girlfriend stage in my life. I want a wife.

ALICA raises an eyebrow, then turns her head.

ALICIA

Mmm.

And here is my car. It was nice talking to you. Thanks again for going with me to lunch. And for the book.

DON

No problem. Have a great evening.

ALICIA tips the driver and turns back towards DON before she gets into the car.

ALICIA

And how would you know when you have found your wife?

DON smiles.

DON

A man's intuition.

ALICIA drives off and DON immediately texts her.

DON

[Text]

That was the short answer. I'll need a couple of

pages to explain what I
mean.

ALICIA

[Text]

Well let me know when the
pages are ready.

INT. DON'S HOUSE. LIBRARY - NIGHT

DON is in his home library reading his emails when he comes across MICHELLE's email.

DON reads the email with deep focus.

After DON reads the email he sits and stares at the computer for a while. Then he opens a word document and begins to type.

INT. ALICIA'S BEDROOM - NIGHT

ALICIA is in bed reading *Selfish Sunday* when she receives a text from DON.

DON

[Text]
The longer version.
[Text]
[.pdf attachment]

ALICIA

Wow. Looks like it's written in detail. I'll read it after I finish reading the first chapter of this book. I love it already.

Selfish Sundays

Written By

Ethel "Ms. Sunday" Bey

My name is Ethel "Ms. Sunday" Bey. I was born in 1917 in Lake Charles, Louisiana. I am now one-hundred- and-two years young. I am a seamstress, cook, gardener, herbalist, healer, teacher, and psychologist. I'm most known for my knowledge of plants, which was passed down by my parents. We used traditional methods from our ancestors. I was raised on a farm in South Carolina where we were self-sufficient. My mother was my teacher and my doctor. I naturally picked up gardening and cooking by helping my mother prepare meals. As I got older, I realized that by being a cook, my mother was also being a doctor. My mother's Louisiana style meals were filled with healing herbs. Teas during breakfast was also remedies to rid our bodies of sickness. Before modern medicine, we survived by knowledge of the land.

I learned meditation by sitting under the trees. I would spend hours observing nature and being one with it. I also learned a lot from watching animals. They were created with a natural instinct to care for their young. I watched the animals care for their sick young and began to take notes. I would experiment with the plants that they would use and began to understand their healing powers. By the time that I was an adult, I had my own healing

I attended college at Spelman College and took my recipes with me. While in college, I adopted the name 'Ms. Sunday' for my teachings on Sunday. When we were free from our studies we would gather and meditate. With all of the turmoil that was going on around us, many students needed an outlet. I taught the ladies the peace that I had learned on the farm. In time, they would ask me about the plant based drinks that I would drink. After a period of time, I was the teacher, mentor, healer, and psychologist for many of my peers. I had a God given talent before any man would certify me in an area. They called me 'Ms.' because they said that I had an old spirit.

Healing is not just a physical process. It is also a mental and spiritual process. Our body can't heal properly if our mind is not in a stable place. It was important for me and the ladies to laugh, dance, and meditate as a part of the process. We also had to be spiritual in order to trust that God gave us plants for healing. We are in relation with everything of the earth.

As the Mothers of the earth, it's important for us to protect our womb. Everyone enters the world through our matrix. It's important for us to be at peace so that we can limit the passing of our traumas to the next generation. It's important that we limit the passing of our disease as well. There is great responsibility that comes with being a woman.

In my years, I've seen a lot of people come and go. I've seen people spending their whole youth chasing materials and neglecting health. I've seen health turn into those same people's greatest expense toward the end of their lives. Health should always be our top focus. Health is our greatest asset.

Search For Yourself

If you had to please a duplicate of yourself, how would you go about doing so? First, you would have to get to know this person in order to know what they like. This same tactic goes for yourself. In order to get to know yourself, you have to go back to your natural state by getting rid of the layers that the world has attached to you. The world is full of subliminal messages that are affecting us without us consciously knowing. A lot of our decisions are made by these same messages coming to the surface of our thoughts. Once we pull back the layers of the world, we start to differentiate between the things that we want versus what the world has influenced us to like. It's kind of like a woman cutting her hair for the first time, stripping herself from the beauty standards of the world. This awareness wakes us up from the dream of unconsciousness.

You have to know and believe that you are a Devine being. Research your history and see how much power is in your DNA. There is enough information in your DNA to connect you back to the beginning of time. You are connected to everything great that exists. When we know who we are, we also know who we aren't. Once we know our worth, we won't accept anything that doesn't reflect that worth. We also won't participate in any activity that doesn't reflect that worth. A lot of the negative things that we participate in is a reflection of how we look at ourselves. We also have the same mental state with materials. We take care of the things that is considered to be worth more.

A part of being at peace is creating a peaceful environment. Peace is not necessarily going to find you; you have to find peace. This begins every day that you wake up, and ends every night that you go to sleep. Your mind is your biggest environment because it's where you spend the most time. The first step in peace is being able to control your mind. Many of our problems only exist in perspective, if not all. Struggle for us is a blessing in another place in the world. Once we have tamed our mind, we will be able to find the silver lining in any tragedy.

ALICIA reads the first chapter then closes her book. She reaches and turns off her reading lamp.
ALICIA closes her eyes for a few minutes, then opens them again and grabs her phone to read DON'S text.

[Text]

Every day in my life I strive for progression. Progression means accepting and working to achieve knew challenges. I never found comfort in the same place, so I never wanted to be doing the same things forever. With accepting challenges, comes growth. With growth, comes a new form of us. This causes our mind to adapt to the person that we become and the skills that we obtain. When I say that I'm past the girlfriend stage in my life, I mean that I grew past committing to the idea of a girlfriend. Many times we do end up achieving our goals, so if my goal is to constantly have a girlfriend then that's what I'll end up having. I just consciously changed my goal. I mean that I've mastered that level of life and I'm ready for a new challenge. *(The contractual debate of marriage is another book so let's stay on the idea of a life commitment; contractual or not.)*

We always talk about a woman's intuition, but what about a man's intuition? If indeed it's a man's duty to find a wife, then he should be intuitively equipped to do so; blessed by his creator. Many people confuse not acting on our intuition with not knowing. Many times we know when a woman is eternally compatible with us and still choose not to act on it due to us not being ready. Unfortunately for me, I had this intuition a little too early, when I wasn't able to fill the shoes of a husband. This caused me to not be compatible, regardless of my intuition. Many times we are focused on the basics of relationships. We think about romance and faithfulness, but being a husband or wife means so much more. There are many skills that we need to be successful. The difference is, now I am confident in my skills.

The first part of the journey is facing ourselves. Looking into the mirror and confronting our flaws. Figuring out what characteristics about us were causing us to fail and deciding whether we want to change them or not. Once we have an outline of the things that we need to work on, then we can work towards overcoming them. Then we start to master new skills that will help us in the future. Once we've groomed ourselves, then we can go back out into the world and try again. Many times we look at failure as something bad when it is the first steps to anything great. I don't get up and ride my bike through trails thinking about the times that I fell off as a child, in training to get to this point. A part of healing is embracing our failures as stepping stones. I genuinely praise every woman of my past for making me into the man that I am today. I love every woman of my past, and I'll say that in any room. They were my teachers. There is no journey without them. To understand a person, you have to understand their journey. You have to know how far they have come to understand the result of today. Every decision that I make is a conscious decision based on what I've been through or where I am trying to go.

Once we've groomed ourselves into a better person, we usually go on a journey to find someone who has done the same work in themselves. If not, someone that we feel that is worthy of helping to get to where we are. The hardest part is finding someone to go on an eternal journey with. This is the point that I am at now. In reference to photography, the value is like the difference between digital and film. In our learning stages we are loaded with a digital camera with unlimited memory. We are just taking shots and praying for one good one out of the thousand shots. Then we are editing our mistakes and smoothing out our flaws before we show the world our finished product. The next level is like film photography and requires more skill. If you have an important shot and you only have one film left, you are going to hold more value to that shot. You are going to make sure that it's perfect before you click. There is no editing. You have to accept the shot as you took it. This is the patience of the next level. In understanding this, why do people look at patience as a bad thing? Why can't people take the time to be sure? Is this the cause of so many people's failure?

I think that a part of our misunderstanding is that we don't genuinely want to have a successful commitment. We don't genuinely want to be our healthiest self. We just want to get by, hide our flaws, and have someone accept it. We find it weird when someone knows their value and stands firm on what they accept.

A part of my patience and failure is due to my overstanding of people. When you are blessed with a vision to see through people it also shows you their negatives. I see a lot of negatives in the dating community that I don't want to be a part of. Being a part of them means going back to the person that I was before. Going backwards means that my sacrifices were in vain. I'm too happy in my today to go back to yesterday. I'm only allowed to be happy with yesterday as the person that I was at that time. I'm only allowed to be happy in the future as the person that I need to be in the future. Unfortunately, our growth doesn't wait on our surroundings, so we have to migrate where our mind goes.

I always say that we only know what we've been through and I've been through a lot. This allows me to overstand actions that I've seen before. They say that game recognizes game and I have a ton of it, so there aren't many things that anybody can get pass me. The only way to be successful with me is to be 100% authentic. I played the game and got the trophy for it, but in judging the person that they see today, some think that they can run game; and are confused when they are denied. I think that women are so used to men being cliché that they use the same game on every man. If game was to be ran on me, I request for it to be at my level of intellect. A quote that we say amongst men is that, "A killer is always the quiet one in an argument because he knows what he is capable of." With that being said, I don't participate in a game because I know what I am capable of. I am effortlessly a master in romance and can use it for evil on any day.

A part of my overstanding is being raised by women. Women are my comfort zone. I grew up the only male in a house full of women. I've seen women grow from infants to adulthood. I've seen women laugh, cry, tell the truth, and lie. I've seen women fall in and out of love. I've been a part of conversations that can only exist in an intimate environment of women. This gave me an overstanding. In saying that, a lot of games are gullible to me; and any sight of game shows that a person isn't ready for the next level. The best game is no game at all.

The biggest hurdles that I face now is compatibility and availability. We have to understand that everyone isn't compatible with us. We won't like everyone, and everyone won't like us. Even when we like a person, things have to be mutual. Many fail in trying to grow into liking a person. If you are willing to take that gamble with your heart, then praises to you. I'm not willing to take that gamble with my time. Either I like you or not. Either you like me or not. Rejection is something that we have to embrace with life. We don't have to submit to rejection, but we can embrace it. Other compatible women aren't available in that exact moment. Many times you meet people and they show interest, but then you can tell that they have something else going on. They try to juggle both until they know that you are the right one. Then they can drop the current person that they are with. I'll never understand or agree with that. You have to go through the isolation that I went through. You have to go through the healing. I'm not allowing anyone to jump from relationship to relationship. I'm not building a home on another man's foundation. Plus, I've been that man that was left in that manner, so it sits different with me.

Maybe as a man I will never understand some things that women do. I've seen many women settle for a man. Maybe it is because of his lack of, or because her standards are far beyond what she attracts. Whatever the reason, this causes her to be in a relationship that she doesn't want to be in. She stays in this relationship praying for the day that someone comes along and saves her. When in actuality she should save herself. I've played every position, and that's a game that I don't want to play. I don't want to be in love with someone that doesn't want me. I don't want to be in love with someone that I don't really want. I definitely don't want to come save someone from their relationship. I've seen the best fall for temptation in this situation. A great woman that I've never seen a flaw in, panties dripped on me in hopes that I save her from her relationship. As bad as I wanted to use her, with no intentions of saving her, I didn't. I didn't because I respected her. I didn't because I refuse to put that energy into the world. I didn't because I refuse to stop the blessings of my next relationship by living in the paranoia of bad karma. Then I knew that my morals were bigger than lust. The other side of it is that these are the same actions that get men killed. This sloppiness. I don't know how it is where everyone else is from, but men die for women everyday where I'm from. In an age where everyone has multiple partners, drama is inevitable. To have a break from this drama is a blessing. Peace to me is being sure in one person.

In conclusion, I am a person that believes in independence and chooses not to entertain the usual relationship debates. Who doesn't care about someone saying that they aren't cooking until they are married because I can cook for myself. A person who has a lot of love in his life that doesn't have to beg for love from the world. A person that doesn't need a partner to survive. I face temptation every day and there are plenty of people that I wish that I could have quick moments with, but my goal is greater than this temptation. Even if I fail at my goal, I'm good with saying that I tried. I tried to do things in a way that I felt was right.

My goal is a relationship with someone that I am compatible with. A person that is willing to overcome the challenges of life with me. A person that I don't mind being isolated in a blank room with. If we can enjoy each other in this room, then we can enjoy each other any place in the world. Materials and accomplishments are not our reason for existing. Our love is our reason and those things are just a compliment to us. A person that supports where I am and where I am trying to go. A person that I respect. A person that I genuinely think is beautiful. A person that will take the time to overstand me. A person that genuinely supports my passions because they are things that I love. A person that is honest, genuine, smart, and loyal. Most importantly, a person that is always walking as a Queen and is able to raise Kings and Queens.

Once I dated a mirror and I didn't like it;
so I had to change.
I actually fell in love with it;
But it was a mirror so I knew the games.

What I mean by a mirror, is dating someone who is equally yoked with you to a level that it shows you your strengths and weaknesses. Many people go around with the same narrative of what their partners did wrong in a relationship, but never take a chance to address themselves. A lot of times it's hard to judge ourselves, but other people can show us what we don't like about ourselves; and she was that for me.

I've been hurt early in love so after that I always wanted to have the upper hand. So many times I dated people who wanted me more than I wanted them. It was a safe place for me. In relationship debates I would make excuses for the things that I've done and use mind manipulation to continue to do things that I needed to change in order to be a healthy partner. Their love for me would usually allow me to have my way, leaving no room for change. A lot of times we can use people's love for us as a weapon against them; but God stopped me in my tracks when *it* brought me a mirror.

When we are struck by something without expecting it, it impacts us more. Love can strike us like a fist or a car crash; leaving us no time to brace ourselves for its impact. Neither of us was expecting love. We didn't even think that we would connect the way that we did. We usually judge people by their appearance, and neither of us was limited to our appearance. We were way more complex than that, so we never expected the person that we were introduced to. Truthfully, I think that we both just wanted something to casually do.

Through the first conversation, I knew that I had been wrong about her. I only focused on her beauty, so I never took into consideration what her mind was like. We sat and talked for hours and really related to each other. A lot of times we go into relationships expecting to put our best self forward. Then we meet some people and realize that we can just let go and be ourselves. We don't have to be perfect because they aren't looking for perfection. We understood each other. I realized that she was a lot like me. We both grew up in hard environments, but elevated to better. We both had big families. We both were into deep conversations and had the ability to exchange on a deep level. We both were uncomfortably honest. I've always been really honest with people because I never really cared about losing people. People would always tell me that I'm too honest, but I finally got a taste of my own medicine. At first the honesty is cool, but when you start to have feelings for a person it gets annoying. To accept someone for who they really are is really a battle. Often times we rather commit to the one that's far worse, but hides their flaws. I was very transparent with her and she had to accept my truth. She was very transparent with me and I had to accept hers. The only problem is, deep down we didn't. When really our truth was similar. Here are two people that are used to having their way with many people and they can't seem to shake each other.

I've always been entertained by many women and I was a master of putting a cast iron over my heart. She has always been entertained by many men and was used to being overwhelmed by a man's attention. I got her off balance when I didn't show her much attention. She was confused and addressed her concern. On the other hand, I was very interested, but I have never been the type to chase anyone. She was used to being on defense, so having to play offense was uncomfortable for her. Through conversation, we both knew that we were entertaining other people, but that didn't stop us from getting closer.

Since there was no title, I was free to do what I wanted; but I got to the point where no one else satisfied me. That's another level, when you want to do something instead of being policed into faithfulness. Though both of us were attached to each other, we never gave up all of the other people that we've been hanging on to for years. We always had that backup. Even when we began to hide, we knew, because we were one in the same. We've been so comfortable in the way that we were doing things that we didn't want to give it up. Whether it was just entertainment from other people or manipulating opportunities, we were holding on to it. That back up kind of gave us leverage. Investing everything in one person makes us vulnerable. We didn't want the vulnerability, but love requires that. Yes, you may lose it all, but that's the high risk gamble that love requires.

In the end, I realized what I needed to change about myself. I understood that if I wanted to attract a wife then I had to change myself. I had to be authentic in anything that I portrayed to be. I had to work on myself to be a man that is worthy of the title husband. My change required isolation. It required me to detox and remove myself from the temptation that I was used to. Through this isolation, I gained more time to invest in myself. I think that we do deserve mirrors. Mirrors are karma. Us getting back what we put out. Now I'm ready for my mirror.

ALICIA wipes the tears off of her phone screen. She just realized that she had been silently crying.

After you've told all of your stories,

next comes a first impression.

-Dushawn Banks

To have someone that **understands** your *soul*, is a different **level** of pleasure.

-Dushawn Banks

In life, hopefully we continue to grow into **greater** versions of ourselves. May we understand that people are put in our lives as *stepping* stones to get us to the greater individual that we are supposed to be. May we understand that some people are only relevant in the **moment** and only compatible with the individual that we are today; or were yesterday. Though it's okay to love many people, we have to know that everyone can't come with us to our greater selves. We will grow and change, and begin to understand the importance of compatibility. God won't make everyone compatible with us, because many times we take abundance for *granted.* One day we will find someone that's on the same page as us. They will be mentally and spiritually in tune with where we are. They will be intellectually and emotionally where we are. What once was strange to everyone else, will be an *'I understand'* from this individual. Some will never allow themselves to find this compatibility, while others will find it many times. If you ever find compatibility, never take it for granted. Even if you have to let go of everything to hold on to it.

We grow up following people at first because that's our only way of learning. As we follow people, we adopt some of their politics or the politics of the world. Hopefully we grow into a space where we begin to think on our own. There are moments in life where we erase politics. One of these moments is death. In this moment we realize what's really important.

Another important time in our life is love. We have all of these politics surrounding love, but politics is only opinion. Majority rule is only the majority opinion. We usually go on a journey with multiple people before we get to our final love, or we go on a journey with one person. I think the journey is beautiful because we can learn some things along the way, so when we get to our true love, we are able to love them correctly. When we begin the journey, it doesn't take much to satisfy us, but as we grow it takes much more. When we are on ground level, things are a bit saturated, but as we grow past the people that we began with, it can become very isolating. Some of these people include our past loves. When we don't have things in abundance we appreciate them more; This includes people and time. That's why I said that in the moment of death we think from a different level. When we were young, out of ignorance, we thought that we would have many people to choose from. We also thought that we had all of the time in the world. After a couple of breakups, we realize the importance of being compatible with someone. There are many more reasons not to like a person than there is to like a person, so we go through a stage where no one satisfies us. Then one day the right person appears and we feel a breath of fresh air. We don't have to train them to do anything because they are already compatible with us. We can finally have conversations about things that we kept to ourselves because no one understood; an outlet that is also great for our mental health. What was frustrating became really simple, and falls right into place. In this moment, we realize that all of the walls that we had were excuses. We made many excuses with the people before, but for the right one, we find ourselves open to everything. We are willing to climb mountains for this person. We are willing to give up all politics. We drop all walls, because we know how hard it is to find this. We understand that our happiness is more important than anything.

Film Synopsis

Title: Selfish

Writer: Dushawn Banks

Selfish is a transforming love story centered on a romance between an entrepreneur, Don Forbes, and a therapist, Michelle Brown. They have a romantic relationship while trying to navigate through their twenties; balancing their relationship, career, and self-care. Michelle Brown is constantly in thought of staying with the past or embracing future relationships. The job of a therapist and mom requires her to be selfless, but that changes when she is around Don. Don has a natural product business which specializes in self-care products. As she moves closer to Don she also moves closer to self-care. It's a war between fantasy and reality, investment and breakthrough, or stability and possibility. A young woman that thought she had the perfect relationship only to realize that happiness is more than having security. What started as innocent payback, turned into her thinking about life with someone else. She is a chess player and has many years invested in her relationship, so she has to juggle both until she chooses the best option. Don says all of the right things and takes her mind off of her career and life in general. This starts to bother her because he shows no interest in her personal life. She is confused on his intentions because he is also weighing his options by juggling another relationship. They are in sync mentally and sexually. His lifestyle meets her standards for the moment, but he isn't stable in the way that she wants him to be. He doesn't have a degree or a cooperate career like the man that she is used to, but she is comfortable with him. He never showed her instability, but she isn't taking any chances. Instead of choosing sides, she just juggles both for as long as she can. She keeps her innocence with both men throughout this time while putting just as much focus on her career. Her ex tries to repair their already broken relationship, but going back would make her seem like a liar. Plus, too much damage has as already been done. She has loyalty to both sides, so she uncovers little information of her true reasoning behind her actions. Maybe she isn't misleading either. Maybe she is just moving in her own way. Maybe she is giving as much commitment as she is being given. Maybe she is finally putting herself first. They are at war with their own perception. Don Forbes moves to Los Angeles to peruse a career and they lose touch. Sparks in their relationship enkindle when they meet again at an event that Michelle is speaking at. Shortly after, Don has a therapy session at Michelle's new wellness office and they have closure.

One day in the future we're going to look back and miss this day. Cherish the moment.

-Dushawn Banks

EXT. BRICE HOTEL - DAY

About Author

Dushawn Banks (born in Savannah, Georgia, 1987) is an American author, writer, director, photographer, and poet. He is the author of three books entitled 'Love, Pain, & Perception', 'Made with Love', and 'Selfish'. Banks has an innovative style of writing, mixing romance and psychology. Banks wrote his first body of work at the age of 14. It was a short screenplay inspired by his favorite movies of the 1990's. The 90's Golden Era of black art inspired the renaissance man within him. Through music he learned poetry, photography, editing, and directing. Banks evolved as a writer, inspiring his own style. Banks' remarkable style is met with warm reception by his readers. Professionally Banks continues to evolve, writing and directing screenplays to bring his stories to life.

Long Live Craig James Franklin Sr.

October 4, 1986 - June 20, 2019

Throughout the year that it took me to write this book, my friend, who I consider a brother, was battling cancer. It was a very tough year because we all were going through this for the first time. We never thought that this would be our battle in our thirties so it was very unexpected. I've always appreciated life, but this made me appreciate life more. We never know when it will be our time to exit. We have to make every day purposeful. I've always been into health, but it made me take a closer look into health. I'll always be an advocate for health on a physical, mental, and spiritual level.

I'll remember Craig as one of the most genuine people that I know. He had a great heart and a big smile. He would take the shirt off of his back and give it to the people that he loves. Though I never seen anyone go through as much pain as he did, I never seen anyone handle it so gracefully. He would never want his family to cry. He handled everything with strength. He believed in being a real man. He left behind two kids and I know that his spirit is still with them.

The last thing that I told my brother was, "I love you." Love forever. You left us on your 32nd year. This is my 32nd year now and I dedicate this whole year to you. May your name travel throughout the world everywhere that mine goes.

Dear Dushawn Banks,

I just finished reading this story and I want to say that it is amazing. At first I thought that it was something that the world would only be entertained by, now I think that it is a story that the world needs. In the year that it took you to finish this book, I can see the shift in your mental state. The ups-and-downs that we have during the course of a year allowed you to write from a genuine place, and your words reflect that. I'm proud of your growth as an artist. I'm happy that you decided to fully walk in the shoes of an artist, regardless of the world's opinion. These are the shoes that you are made to walk in. You are finally walking in your purpose. Whatever success that you have in the future, you deserve. This has been a long journey, but you stayed the course. You didn't compromise who you are for any quick success. When the world slammed their doors on you, you created your own door. You went through every emotion, but you never gave up. When others were out having fun, you were writing. Some days you wondered if you were wasting your time chasing a purpose, but that fire in you never allowed you to quit. When others didn't believe in you, I believed in you. You were born into a system, but you decided to create your own system. You created the life that you wanted. You didn't just want a better life, you worked for it. The discipline that you showed me in these last couple of years is unmatched. You showed me and God that you are really the man that you say you are. You are a born leader. You shine in any room. I just want to say that I'm proud of you again, and I love you.

Sincerely,

Dushawn Banks

Selfish started as a poem written on April 22, 2014, and published on June 19, 2016 in the book *Love, Pain, & Perception*. When *Love, Pain, & Perception* was released, readers were vocal about the stories that intrigued them. The top story talked about was a story written fictionally. I never wanted to be a fictional writer, but this showed me reader's interest in fiction. Fiction allows us to talk about controversial topics with ease. This is where I found the value in fiction.

I would continually write the story in my mind, but I never put it on paper until 2017. In 2017 I started writing the opening scene in book format. I wrote a few pages and lost interest in it. In 2018 I wrote the ballroom scene in screenplay format. I wrote two pages and posted them online to see if readers would be interested in reading a book in screenplay format. To my surprise, it gained a lot of attention. This gave me the motivation that I needed to keep writing.

This was five years in the making and now I'm happy to be finished. I'm sure they do exist, but I've never seen books written in this format. I've heard about many writer's screenplays being written and put on the shelf by Hollywood. Hopefully this opens the door for more writers taking this route with their art.

If you enjoyed this book, please share it with someone else.

Thank you for your support.

Made in the USA
Columbia, SC
27 November 2021

49864484R10198